On
Noah's Ark

On Noah's Ark

Shem's Story

CLAIRE F GRIFFITHS

THE CHOIR PRESS

First published in the United Kingdom in 2019 by
The Choir Press

ISBN 978-1-78963-082-4

For my grandsons

Toby, Otto and Reuben Shaw
Tom, Edward and Ben Griffiths

Grateful thanks to editor Jackie King, friends and readers Tai Lichtensteiger, Richard Hann and David Prosser for their suggestions and encouragement. Not forgetting Lilly Bell for her cover picture.

Contents

Noah Who?

Where Did the Story of Noah Come From?

❖

The extraordinary biblical story of Noah and the Flood has been told for more than 5,000 years. It was originally recorded in Genesis, the first book of the Old Testament of the Bible, which has been translated from the original Hebrew again and again over thousands of years. In each translation the essential features of the Noah story have remained largely unchanged. But what is the Bible, the most influential book in the English-speaking world, and where did it come from? Who wrote it and when and how has it affected us?

The Old Testament was originally written in Hebrew over 4,000 years ago during the Early Bronze Age and compiled over a period of roughly 1,000 years. Its contents range from laws, history, songs, poetry, philosophy, letters and predictions. The Bible as a whole was originally recorded on scrolls and Jewish tradition has it that Moses wrote the first five books of the Hebrew Bible (The Torah), which include the accounts of the Creation and the Flood. After him there were additions by various authors who wrote about events contemporaneously.

Royal scribes recorded matters of state or history, priests were responsible for religious matters and the prophets recorded their own prophecies and their confrontations with royalty. The biblical scrolls were originally kept in the city of Jerusalem, until it was destroyed by the Babylonians in 586BC. Fortunately, many of the scrolls were saved by the exiles and taken to safety where, some-time later under the leadership of the priest and scribe Ezra, they were organised and restored to their original state as far as was possible. Some 30 years or so later, the texts were returned to the rebuilt Jerusalem, where additional works were added to make up the Old Testament or Hebrew Bible as it is known today.

The New Testament was written much later by the Apostles and describes the birth and life of Jesus in the time of Herod Antipas, when the lands previously known as Israel were under Roman rule. It continues with the spread of Christianity, which is seen as a threat to the Roman rulers and the Jewish authorities and ends with the Book of Revelations, which warns that the wicked will get their comeuppance, the kingdom of God will be established and that Paradise will be restored.

Following Alexander the Great's extraordinary trail of conquests 356BC–323BC, Greek culture pervaded much of the known world. In the near East, as elsewhere, Greek had become the common language. And, with the demise of the Hebrew language, many Jews were no longer able to read their own scriptures.

Around 250BC, 70 scribes worked to translate the content of the scriptures, the Torah, into Greek. Working independently, it is said their translations were all virtually identical, proving that the content of the resulting translation was reliable.

Later, additional Jewish historical and religious writings known as the Apocrypha were added as well. At the time these were revered and regarded as valuable additions but 150 or so years later they were rejected by a group of scholars who gathered at the city of Yavneh near Jerusalem; they decreed that the Apocrypha were not divinely inspired and thus should not be regarded as part of the Bible.

By this time many of the early Christians were using the Septuagint, the Greek translation, which included the Apocrypha and they continued to regard them as authoritative parts of the Bible.

The matter was addressed again in 391AD when Pope Damasus I commissioned the scholar St Jerome to translate parts of the Bible into Latin, which was commonly used at that time.

The result was the Vulgate version of the Bible, which was widely used for the next 1,000 years. It was based on Jerome's own translations of the Hebrew Old Testament and Greek texts of the New Testament, which were available to him at the time. He omitted the Apocrypha, which caused much dissent.

By the time of the Protestant Reformation in the 16th century, the additional books had been removed from most versions of the Protestant Old Testament, but the Apocrypha are still largely accepted as part of the Bible by the Catholic and Eastern Orthodox Church.

Having been translated from Hebrew to Greek and then to Latin, it was inevitable that there should be a call for translations that could be understood not only by the clergy and the highly educated, but also by ordinary Christians. Partial translations of the Vulgate Bible from Latin to English had begun only a few hundred years after it had been published against much opposition.

John Wycliffe helped to translate the Old Testament from the Vulgate into English and many words from the Latin became a part of the English language through the translations.

In 1520 William Tyndale, the Protestant reformer, made the first translation of the New Testament from Greek to English. By 1526, when he was living in exile for his beliefs, he had also translated the Old Testament from the original Hebrew, helped by the radical German theologian and Augustinian monk, Martin Luther. Luther had produced the first translation of the entire Bible in German in 1522.

Although Tyndale's translation is renowned for the beauty of its language, he was burnt alive at the stake in 1536 for the heresy of his work and the late Wycliffe's bones were exhumed and burnt for the heresy of his translating.

The first translation of the entire Bible, both the Old and the New Testament, into English, was Miles Coverdale's version in 1535; he used Tyndale and Luther's work and previous Latin translations.

Not surprisingly, the next translator, John Rogers, was more circumspect about claiming public authorship of his work. His version was known by his pseudonym as the 'Thomas Matthew Bible', in which he included some of Tyndale and Coverdale's previous translations. Unfortunately for him, he was still put to death.

After this, Coverdale revised his original translation, which was to be the first authorised version of the Bible in English. On the order of Henry VIII who was then head of the Church of England, a copy was to be placed in every church in the Kingdom.

The next important version was the Geneva Bible, a revision of Coverdale's Bible that was produced by Protestants in exile from Henry's eldest daughter, the Catholic Queen Mary – or 'Bloody Mary' – in 1560. This was the translation Shakespeare would have heard in church and his style owes much to the rhythm of the words in this version.

The Geneva Bible was the first edition to have numbered verses and was the translation that was taken to America by the Pilgrim Fathers in 1620.

In 1604 King James I commissioned yet another version of the Bible which was finally completed in 1611; this was the one that was to become the most beloved of all. Its production was not solely for religious reasons, rather political ones to persuade his subjects to be loyal to their King. His mother, Mary Queen of Scots, had been a staunch Catholic; the English were Protestant, so on his succession he had to try to unify the two kingdoms with their disparate faiths. He failed and by the 1640s civil war broke out, with the words of the Bible being quoted as justification by both sides.

Meanwhile in America, in 1776, when the Declaration of Independence was signed, Thomas Paine, who had stimulated debate in his widely read pamphlet 'Common Sense', quoted the Bible saying, "All men are created equal". In this he conveniently forgot the fact that much of America's wealth was created by the work of African slaves.

From 1861 to 1865 the American Civil War was fought, lasting almost four years to the day; 750,000 people died and the Bible was provided to the soldiers for inspiration and comfort. Some even had their weapons embossed with the words "I am the light of the world".

As well as the Southern states' desire for independent recognition there was the problem of slavery. Some tried to justify this by harking back to the passage in Genesis where Noah cursed Cain's sons to be slaves.

Conversely, at around this time there were remarkable developments amongst the black slaves in the Southern states of America. They had begun to organise themselves, finding inspiration from the words of the Bible in their struggle for freedom. They held 'invisible meetings' where literate slaves would read to the others. They sang gospel songs and the language of the Bible was an important unifying factor for them all, as they had originally come from many different parts and tribes in Africa and so often could not understand each other in their original tongues.

One of the most inspirational characters in the struggle against slavery was the remarkable Harriet Tubman (1820–1913), an illiterate black slave who worked with incredible bravery and fortitude for abolition of slavery. Tubman led slaves from the Southern states to safety in the North and in Canada on the so-called 'underground railway', which was a network of people who, at great danger to themselves, would shelter and hide slaves during their journey to safety.

The Bible's influence has not just been philosophical and social; it was the genesis of modern science. Sir Francis Bacon (1561–1626), the philosopher and statesman, whose methods of scientific research were hugely influential in the foundation of modern scientific enquiry, was an advocate of the use of nature and the scriptures, in order to discover the mind of God. He was called by some one of the most brilliant men who ever lived; the manner of his death, however, may belie his common sense (he caught a chill while researching the possibility of cold inhibiting putrefaction by stuffing a chicken carcass with snow).

Sir Isaac Newton (1643–1727), the renowned mathematician and physicist, was also strongly religious and is regarded as one of the most brilliant scientists of all time. He revered the Bible and accepted its account of the Creation. He was one of the foremost members of the Royal Society, created to the glory of God the Creator to promote knowledge of the natural world through observation and experiment, or as it is known today, science. At the time of its formation in 1661, most scientists were religious.

Michael Faraday (1771–1867) was another enormously influential scientist carrying out seminal work on electro-magnetism, of whom it was said, "A strong sense of the unity of God and nature pervaded Faraday's work."

Whereas science was originally driven by man's desire to know the mind of God, today it is not without irony that a number of contemporary scientists are amongst the most vociferous sceptics. But there are still many things that confound them.

In the 1960s the physicist Peter Higgs postulated the existence of the so-called 'God Particle', a particle (or particles) that might give mass to others and explain the mystery of the Creation. But to date, the first cause has yet to be explained. And there had to be a first cause. The Big Bang theory is now discredited and so we may have to accept there are some things science may never explain.

Art is another area in which the Bible has been massively influential, providing a huge source of inspiration for artistic illustration through sculpture, painting and music. Many of the most beautiful works of art in the world are on biblical themes (sceptics may say the wealthy who commissioned them were merely hoping to burnish their religious credentials). The renowned art critic and social commentator John Ruskin (1819-1900), who had a religious upbringing, said, "The purpose in the heart of every great artist is not to choose something that will please, but to give expression to something that profoundly moves him and by which he desires to move others."

The words of the Bible lucidly disclose the wishes of God and point to the often wayward nature of man. They have helped provide a civilising effect and offered to some a respite from the harsh realities of life. Although contrasting religious beliefs have also been at the root of many violent conflicts, the Bible's influence is immeasurable.

When?

The story of Noah and the flood has endured for more than 5,000 years and is beloved by children and adults alike.

For the first 1,000 years the story was passed down the generations by word of mouth before being written down in Genesis, the first book of the Old Testament, 4,000 years ago. Written communication was far behind people's ability to create fire, build boats, make weapons such as bows and arrows, sew clothes, fashion metal objects and conceive art.

It is the story of an extraordinary family with an enormous task to complete against great odds, namely, at the command of God, gathering together and looking after a huge number of animals to save them from a watery death.

The development of the very first writing in cuneiform script by the ancient Babylonians enabled the words of the great prophet Moses to be inscribed on clay tablets. It is Moses's account of the flood that we read today, an account written down for the first time 1,000 years after the flood is said to have occurred.

It was Moses who freed the Israelites, God's chosen people, from slavery under the Egyptians. Disappointingly, the Israelites continued to believe in many deities, so Moses received from God the covenant of the Ten Commandments, which were a list of moral guidelines to help the freed Israelites live a moral and fulfilling life.

There is considerable scepticism about the veracity of the flood story and debate about whether or not it should be regarded as true or allegorical. Similar stories of a great flood are told by many different cultures all over the world and are important in Islamic and Christian scriptures.

As geologists and sceptics point out, it has been virtually impossible for theologians to verify the early parts of the Old Testament as it records no known historical events until around 1,000BC, where it corresponds with other sources *to describe King David (1010–970BC) creator of the house of Judah, uniting Israel and making Jerusalem the capital.*

In North America for instance, geological evidence points to glaciation rather than flooding as an explanation for areas such as the Great Plains, where legend has it that the massive erosion and flattening of the land was the result of one universal flood. And in the Middle East, geological research shows that most if not all of the present-day deserts were densely forested before flooding and that millions of years of compaction have produced today's rich oil deposits. But this is very far outside the timescale of the biblical flood, which according to the Old Testament took place around 5,000 years ago.

❦

Chapter 1

I t all started one afternoon in the middle of summer, a day like any other, nothing out of the ordinary. The village was quiet, the streets deserted and the temperature, as always at that time of year, was oppressively hot. The slightest movement was enough to make me sweat. On such days I preferred to shelter from the sun in the doorway of our house, hoping to catch even the slightest breeze, while others chose to doze or sit quietly outside in whatever shade they could find. With summer half over, the long leaves of the palm trees surrounding the well hung motionless in the shimmering heat of the day and I sat in the shadows and longed for the cool and the rains of winter.

Our family lived in one of the many small communities along the shores of the great eastern river and eked out a living from the flat and fertile land. On the outskirts of the village there were still a few tent dwellers who lived intermittently nomadic lives, only returning to the village when it was either very hot or very cold. Whether they were any more comfortable in their oiled tents than we were in our clay and rush houses, it was hard to say.

The stifling stillness of that hot afternoon was only broken by an old dog, unsteady on his legs, slowly loping down the side of the main street in the shade, and a few whiskery pigs that in spite of the heat trotted busily along the narrow alleys, stopping here and there to snuffle hopefully for grain husks or, if they were lucky, the odd crust of discarded barley bread.

By this time of day the dung man had long-since been round the village collecting any animal droppings that might attract flies and the heat soon desiccated any other waste that had not been removed or quickly eaten by scavengers. Apart from the dust, the whole village was clean as a bone.

The reeds growing down by the river crackled and split; the grass on the plains was burnt and its fragile sun-bleached roots were struggling to maintain their tenuous hold on the dry earth. In the fields the crop heads of wheat and barley had bowed over and the grain dangled from their stems before some finally dropped to the ground, which meant our bread would be full of grit and the beer would taste muddy, I thought glumly. Our houses were coated with dust inside and out – everything was – and if there was the slightest breeze we had to cover our faces to stop it filling our mouths and eyes. Strangely we didn't think of it as dirt, just dust, we were so used to it at this time of year. If our wives had spent all their days sweeping it up there would still be more, it was simply a fact of life in the summer, along with the heat.

Inside, the women had laid their spindles down, the pottery wheel was still and our fire-pit unused. It was hot enough to bake the pots we made from the river clay simply by laying them out carefully to dry in the sun. No work was done in the fields during the day, although down by the river the odd fisherman might be found threading his nets, feet dangling in the cool, shallow waters of the river. Apart from that no one moved about if they didn't have to. I was certainly in no hurry to do any work; my chores could wait until the cool of the evening and in truth even then I might not have the energy or inclination to do them.

There was no breeze from the plains that day, nor was there any cool air blowing down from the mountains on the far side of the river to make things more pleasant. I couldn't even muster the energy needed for a real dislike of summer on days like this, when it was so punishingly hot. Even the prospect of working on the seemingly endless irrigation channels that we had to dig and clear in the cooler weather would have been preferable to enduring this energy-sapping heat.

Our neighbours were farmers and fishermen who, like us, had given up their nomadic lives and settled in the village, each family cultivating various pieces of land along the river, digging irrigation channels, planting crops, tending a few animals and collecting the plenteous dates, figs and pomegranates that grew untended around us.

We had domestic animals as well – a mule, a few pigs, some sheep and goats – but ours certainly wasn't the finest or the largest flock in the village. We did the best we could with them, all the men of the family taking it in turns to drive the animals far and wide over the nearby plains but, in spite of our efforts, none of them were particularly fine specimens. Our sheep and goats always looked a bit scrawny by comparison with most of our neighbours' animals; our pigs were rather small and our mule was an unruly creature that appeared to greatly resent its role in life as a beast of burden.

As for our dogs, only Japhet's beloved herder obeyed any of the commands he gave it and all the others were virtually wild. We knew very well that they only showed us any allegiance because we fed them. When there was food about they would writhe around us with obsequious gratitude, trying to slip into the house at every opportunity so they could sleep in the cool, undisturbed and safe. So I am being honest, not modest, when I say that we were not renowned for our husbandry skills, rather the opposite in fact.

There was one great benefit to this, though: any particularly fine animals that a villager might have were in danger of being requested by the local priests to provide sacrifices to the various gods and it was supposed to be regarded as a great privilege to be asked. Fortunately for us, apart from handing over a few of Mother's fine-looking hens, we were rarely troubled with such requests.

In the extreme heat at this time of year it was only possible to work in the fields and harvest our crops in the early hours of the day before the sun was up, or in the cool of the evening before sunset. The women spent most of their time inside, spinning and weaving unless it was too hot, only venturing outside to fetch water from the village well or to cook the family meals at dawn and dusk. At those times of the day the heat from the fire didn't raise the temperature inside the houses to unbearable levels, although on days like this, I really don't think it would have made that much difference.

So, back then we were just an ordinary family. None of us was special in any way and I'm sure nobody else thought we were either. Even now I can't really understand why we were 'chosen', other than to get our Father, Noah, on board. A good man was obviously essential, given the reason for the flood in the first place, and he needed to have a family for future procreation and our Father had three married sons. But I suppose it's also fair to say that as a family we were all decent people, not perfect of course, for even Father had his faults, but if we were the best that were available at the time it could explain a lot.

Fortunately, our village and the surrounding land was situated along the well-irrigated banks of the great river in an area that was renowned for its fertility and productivity.

"Only a fool could starve to death here," our old neighbour Ethan used to say.

And he was right. The land was rich and by working hard it was possible for everyone to be virtually self-sufficient. We hardly ever needed to leave the village, although occasionally one or two of us would travel to a larger community where small farmers like us could sell or barter our excess goods. However, with eight of us in the family we used most of our produce ourselves and, if we did ever have a surplus of meat or wool, it was often of rather indifferent quality so we didn't get much for it. We might have done better bartering our crops, which Father and I seemed to have a certain amount of success with, but we never had much to spare. Luckily our wives, Salit and Arisisah in particular, made beautiful pots and bowls which were quite sought after and Nahlat was adept at making necklaces and other adornments when she felt like it.

Back then no one would have described Father as a charismatic man or a natural leader; he was a little taller than the average it is true, but really he was just like everyone else. Admittedly we couldn't help but notice that recently he seemed to have become peculiarly obsessed with living a good and moral life and he didn't keep his thoughts to himself, either. He began to publicly admonish the family, our neighbours and anyone else he could get to listen, telling us all that we should mend our sinful ways or be punished by the wrath of God. This didn't always go down very well, as I'm sure you can imagine.

"Which God would that be then, Noah?" Ethan's son Isaac asked him sarcastically. "The God of the Barley, the God of the Moon, or do you mean the Sun God? Or the River God, perhaps? You have to tell us which God so that we know how to please him."

But Father just said God, not which God. It was as if something had got into him and he began to argue with everyone, even the priests and soothsayers who were used to being regarded as the authorities on all such matters, the only ones people consulted on how to please or appease the numerous Gods. They knew all the important rituals and the times of the year to carry them out and how to read the signs in the entrails of dead animals and how to interpret any odd or unusual happenings. Nothing important was ever carried out without consulting them to check if the signs were auspicious. They played an integral part in everyone's lives and were used to being revered and taken notice of, so they were particularly annoyed with Father for challenging their authority and putting their livelihood in danger. His strange notion of there being only one God contradicted their authority. How could one God possibly be responsible for everything? It was ridiculous, quite impossible, and blasphemous too. "Noah is mad," they said.

But Father would have none of it and persisted in contradicting them: "Not Gods, one God, there is only one God and he speaks to you all through me."

Those words and their apparent arrogance shocked everyone including us, his family; there was simply no precedent for pleasing just one God. We had always believed in many Gods and they all had their own special responsibilities, with rituals and offerings, which had to be carried out at the right time of day, in the right week and the right month of the year to please them. It was accepted by everyone that the priests and soothsayers knew exactly when this was and what to do. How could there possibly be just one God, and since when did any God speak through Noah?

Not surprisingly our neighbours rapidly came to the conclusion that Father was asking for trouble and they didn't want to be associated with his ridiculous belief. For his part Father continued to insist that they were the ones who should be worried if they continued to ignore him. What was certain was that with his radical ideas he had infuriated the local priests and with his predictions of doom and his notion of one God they became his enemies, encouraging everyone to either ignore him, or mock and ridicule him and his ideas.

Yet for all his certainty, so far Father had never told us anything about how the wrath of his God would manifest itself. In fact, if he had told us about the ark back then, this simply enormous boat that we were expected to build ourselves, we too would have thought he was mad. But I'm afraid, like everyone else, we never took much notice of what he said. When he started one of his public outbursts or rants, as Ham's wife Nahlat aptly called them, we either ignored him or laughed at him behind his back, just as our neighbours did. The priests on the other hand fumed with anger at his challenge to their authority. To be honest, we all felt that he was a bit of an embarrassment, especially my brother Ham.

"The family prophet," Ham would say scathingly after one of Father's sermons, mainly to hide his mortification at Father making a show of himself and indeed the whole family. And while I am sure our neighbours must have found him irritating at times, so far I don't think any of them actually thought he was mad.

Subsequently I must admit this opinion did change but, until then, our lives went on very much as normal and Father's predictions had no effect at all.

No one could argue with the fact that lately Father had been acting oddly, increasingly so in fact. But we were still quite unprepared for the strangeness of what happened next. And to say that what he did finally tell us about the wrath of God took us all by surprise would be something of an understatement.

Even now, looking back on that afternoon so many years ago, I can hardly believe it. Or that Father actually got us all to take him seriously. Late that particular afternoon, as the heat of the day cooled a little, he called us all together, none of us knowing why. We listened to him in utter amazement while he told us about his latest command from God – that we must build an enormous boat on which we would all live while the rest of the world around us would be washed away by a disastrous flood.

"What?" asked my youngest brother Japhet looking rather pale.

Father continued, "From my numerous communications with God he has made me aware that the behaviour of men has sorely tried his patience. Most seem to be incapable of acting decently, honestly, respectfully or with kindness."

"Yes, yes, same old stuff," muttered my other brother Ham, swatting away a persistent fly that had been attracted by the beads of sweat on his face.

"And unfortunately," continued my Father, "in spite of all my efforts to warn as many people as possible of God's displeasure, nothing has changed."

"Oh no, not all this again," Ham whispered to me.

"So," Father went on, "So God has entrusted us with a very great task: we have been chosen to save all the creatures that he has created. There is to be a great flood over the whole world and it will be the end of everything and everyone we do not save. We have to build an ark and you, my three sons, your wives, your Mother and I will be the only people on the ark, together with two of the finest examples of every living thing, animal, bird or reptile that cannot survive in water."

"Oh, of course," muttered Ham raising his eyes to the sky.

After this there was a lot of incredulous, angry muttering from the other villagers who had gathered around us to hear what was going on while we, his family, stood there transfixed by what we

16

had just heard. I was so hot by then that I wondered if I was hallucinating and hearing strange things and for quite a while it seemed as if we had all been struck dumb. None of us knew quite how to react or what to say and none of us dared to laugh, not even with astonishment, except for Ham who couldn't quite suppress a snort of derision. But whatever the rest of us thought about Father's plan, we could all see that he was deadly serious about it.

Once the neighbours who had heard Father speaking to us got over their initial shock, it wasn't long before they drifted away and began to spread the news to all our other neighbours and the sound of their laughter echoed around the village. This time not even Mother, who usually supported Father in everything, took his idea well and neither did our wives. And I remember wondering if this was just another of his tall stories, or whether we should actually believe him this time. It was such an outrageous idea that it was hard for any of us to take him seriously and when Ham said, "I think this is the best yet," he was only saying aloud what the rest of us thought.

"Did I hear that correctly?" asked Japhet.

"He has totally lost his mind, hasn't he?" said Ham, who looked as if he was about to stamp his feet with anger.

"All cooped up together, with goats, chickens and dogs, how awful," Mother exclaimed. "Your Father must have gone quite mad."

Ham sarcastically mentioned camels as well, but Japhet said that no boat he had ever seen had been large enough for one camel, let alone a pair of them, so he didn't think Mother need worry.

"Well that's a relief I suppose," said Mother who was looking a little pale by now.

"Honestly, just listen to you all, don't tell me you are taking this seriously?" Ham muttered.

And I remember looking at Father standing there in front of us. The effort of making his announcement to a rather unreceptive audience had obviously made him feel hotter than ever; sweat ran down his face and I saw him wipe his hands on his robes to dry them. He appeared unsure of quite what to do next and in the end he just walked away.

So we had been chosen as the family to restock the world? Suddenly we were faced with an extraordinary dilemma. It wasn't so much that we wondered "why us?" It was more that we found it hard to believe that it really was us, and believe me we were all less than thrilled with the situation for a very long time. We were horrified by the implications of Father's words and this time it wasn't as if we could just ignore him either; he was expecting a major effort on our part to put this extraordinary plan into practice.

I remembered Ham saying to me only that morning that nothing about Father could ever surprise him now. How wrong he was. So there we all stood in the late afternoon heat and trickles of perspiration poured down the inside of my robes as I determinedly jostled over a small patch of shade with a particularly stubborn goat, which resisted all my efforts to move it.

"Actually I don't think he is joking, do you?" Ham whispered to me.

"No, I don't think he is," I replied.

"You don't think he has gone mad?" asked Japhet.

"It had crossed my mind," said Ham.

"No, unfortunately I think he's deadly serious from the look of him, but I suppose he could be mad," I replied.

"Good Lord," muttered Japhet under his breath.

Origins

Various disciplines have contributed to our knowledge of biblical times. Using information gleaned from the Bible, theologians have calculated that the flood described in Genesis took place approximately 5,000 years ago. Using rock formation and sedimentary deposits to learn about the structure of the earth, geologists have estimated that the birth of the universe was approximately 13.5 billion years ago.

Archaeologists say that the first instance of the Homo genus was approximately 250 million years ago, which then evolved into our forebears Homo sapiens less than 250,000 years ago. Naturally there is plenty of scope for academic discussion over the timing and manner of creation itself, let alone the flood.

However, as far as the story of God's creation of Adam and Eve goes, recorded in the Old Testament as taking place several thousand years before the flood, things did not get off to a good start. First there was the incident of the apple in the Garden of Eden. Then Adam's son Cain killed his younger brother Abel and there followed several thousand years of misdemeanours until, so the Bible tells us, God had had enough. He decided to start again, wiping out his whole creation with a terrible flood and keeping only one family and one pair, a male and a female, of each kind of living creature alive.

෬෨෪ൟൟ

Chapter 2

✧

With Father's words ringing in our ears and the prospect of what he had asked us to do buzzing in our brains, we had to seriously question whether anyone in the family was suited to a life of boat-building followed by an intensive stint of animal husbandry on board an ark, floating about goodness knows where? And it wasn't hard to conclude that no, none of us were. Only Ham had had vague aspirations of travelling as a merchant of sorts, bargaining, buying and selling. The rest of us had always been content to live just as we were. I usually spent my time doing odd jobs around the village and helping Father with the crops and Japhet, who was a bit of a loner, was happiest when he was out on the plains herding our flock.

We were in a state of shock about what Father had just told us, what we had to do and what would happen to everyone else. It all seemed so unlikely.

"Somehow I just can't see Ham building a boat can you, Shem?" asked Japhet.

He had a point. I couldn't. Nor, for that matter, could I see Japhet building one either. And although I was the most practical member of the family and could make and mend most things, I knew absolutely nothing about boats, let alone how to build one. Father and I had always taken a particular pride in tending the field crops while Ham and Japhet spent more time looking after our animals. We bartered for fish if we wanted some and had never had any need whatsoever for a boat, or to know anything about boats, apart from how to climb into one for the odd river crossing during the season when the water was high.

Personally I had never had any particular hopes or dreams for the future. I had no desire to travel and I was quite content with my lot. I certainly didn't want to sail about in an ark loaded with both animals and my entire family, all living together in a confined space. I'm quite sure my wife Salit felt the same.

I had known Salit, the daughter of another family in the village, since she was a child and I loved her dearly. She was a practical, easy-going girl, a little on the plain side I have to admit, but I was the first son to get married and I didn't want to risk being rejected. And anyway I was far from handsome myself: I was strong and stocky with weathered skin and donkey brown hair, not darkly good-looking like Ham or delicately built like Japhet, who was pale skinned with Mother's gentle ways. But fortunately Salit seemed happy with the arrangement; she had the kindest of hearts and was a hard worker, always more than willing to help me or anyone else that needed her, so all in all we were well-suited. After Father's speech about the flood, however, Salit's mood darkened in anticipation of what she might be asked to do and I really could-n't blame her. All of us were apprehensive about the future.

As for my youngest brother Japhet, he was never happier than when he was out by himself on the pastures with our flock of sheep and goats, dreaming the days away. Fortunately for him, while on his travels across the plains, he had captured the heart of Arisisah, the youngest daughter of a nomadic tribesman and she was now his wife. Pretty, gentle and undemanding, she was ideal for him. She had an extensive knowledge of herbs and plants and their particular medicinal and flavouring uses, as well as recipes for making beer out of almost anything – skills we were all to be grateful for later on.

My middle brother Ham was tall and handsome, with smooth dark skin and black hair that fell in curls to his shoulders. He was not a potential boat builder and I knew he was not particularly interested in animals. He had never been afraid to say that looking after our flock out on the plains bored him and that tilling fields was worse. When it was his turn to tend the flock he kept himself amused by constantly moving around in search of more congenial surroundings and company, a regime that didn't always coincide with good shepherding practice. On more than one occasion he had let our animals get muddled up with someone else's – most shepherds' worst nightmare – but it didn't seem to bother him.

Ham's wife Nahlat was extremely beautiful, with shining black hair, a slender dark-skinned body and large kohl-rimmed eyes. She had a look that was rather more exotic than that usually seen in our rural community and caused quite a stir when she first arrived. She was the youngest of the six daughters and five sons of a successful farmer from far to the South of our village. He had been far from pleased when Nahlat sulked and begged to be allowed to marry Ham, the handsome son of Noah, who was far from rich by comparison. But he finally agreed on the condition that Father compensated him with half our flock and our only camel. The loss of the sheep and goats was a blow, but the camel was a surly beast, which could spit for several cubits and I for one was more than happy to see it go.

At the time this had been quite a setback for the family, but Japhet had made light of it, joking how typical it was of Ham to choose a wife for whom his Father had to pay a dowry, instead of the more conventional way round. Although she never actually mentioned it, Nahlat may well have been embarrassed by her father's greed and after the marriage she never returned home, although occasionally her brothers would visit us. They were even more insufferably arrogant than Nahlat had been when she first arrived, and had voracious appetites, so their visits were never seen as an occasion for great family rejoicing. While Nahlat was undoubtedly beautiful, her experience of domestic duties seemed to be negligible and I could only wonder at Mother's patience with her.

After Father's shock announcement, only Japhet and I remained calm enough to give it any real consideration and even we wondered if he was really serious. Everyone else was so stunned by what he had said that none of them had a single sensible thought between them. Things became a little more believable when Father gave us some of the specifications and dimensions of the ark which, he told us in all apparent seriousness, had been ordained by God.

"But of course," said Ham rather rudely.

From the measurements he gave us, it didn't take us long to work out that the ark would be unimaginably huge. It was to be made entirely of gopher wood and covered all over with pitch to make it waterproof. When the others heard the details, it set them all off again.

"That can't be right," said Japhet aghast.

"Oh no, not pitch,' Ham groaned. "The smell, the stickiness ... I got some on a good coat once and it never came off. It's awful stuff. Surely, Father can't seriously believe we are capable of building something that size all by ourselves and then covering it all over with pitch, can he? I couldn't knock in a post to tie a donkey to, let alone build a boat or an ark or whatever it is, not even a small one. Anyway, why on earth can't Father's all powerful God or the Gods or whoever, just give us an ark ready-made?"

Japhet looked extremely glum. "I've got to be honest, I'm finding it very hard to believe that all this is happening," he said. "And if it is, can Father possibly have given us the right measurements?"

"Well, I think you're going to have to try to believe it," was all I could think of in reply.

"What on earth's got into Father?" Ham stormed. "Does he really think that we will be able to build a boat that size on some crazy whim of his? None of us has ever done anything like it before. It's just so unreasonable."

But Father insisted that he had got the measurements right and that we really did have to build the boat ourselves; God had decreed this. Who else would he have got to attempt it, anyway? So before long, when people realised that we were going to at least attempt to build the ark, we were not only the laughing stock of our village, but of the entire region as well. It was all extremely embarrassing. And needless to say the local priests and sooth-sayers, who were all furious with Father for contradicting everything they stood for, enthusiastically egged on this mockery. They must have been delighted to see our discomfort and did all they could to add to it.

"But Father," I said, trying to sound diplomatic as the reality – or rather the impossibility – of his plan began to sink in, "you do realise that it will take us years and years to build such a huge boat and that none of us have any previous boat-building experience or have done anything like this before, not even me? And have you taken into consideration what will happen to our crops and animals while we are working on the boat? You know it's a full-time job for us all and now none of our neighbours will help because, not unreasonably to be honest, they all think that we're mad. So if we don't tend to them ourselves, they will starve and so will we. I really don't think that we will have the time to do every-thing."

"And I'm absolutely hopeless at things like that, Father," added Japhet. "You're always saying so, 'all thoughts and not much use at actually doing anything'. I'm just not a very practical man. You know that."

"Oh don't you worry Japhet, there will be plenty for everyone to do," Father reassured him. "Believe me, you will be extremely useful, measuring, working out how many planks we will need, how many wooden dowels, how much food. Your thinking skills will be invaluable."

Ham merely asked Father if he was really serious, which I could see annoyed him.

"Just one wife is it then, Father? I may have to change mine before we go," he said.

Not for the first time I could see Father, who was already irri-tated by our less-than-enthusiastic reaction, wondering how on earth he could have ended up with such an impudent son. Clearly Ham had more than a touch of our Grandfather Lamech about him and some of his ideas must have taken root. I noticed that Nahlat wasn't laughing very much at this and I dare say Ham wouldn't be either when she got him on his own later on.

Right from the start it was obvious that Father really did expect us to build the ark ourselves; there was no arguing with him and none of our attempts to discuss the matter made any difference. He insisted that it had to be built and we were to build it. He was absolutely adamant. And it wasn't only the practical side of building the ark that worried all of us, it was the fate that he had foretold for everyone else that seemed so terrible.

"Well it's not supposed to happen for a very long time by all accounts and things could change a lot by then," was the only consoling thought that I could come up with.

If Father's predictions really came true, what would happen to all the other people, for whom there was to be no place on the ark. What about our neighbours and the nomads and travellers of the plains and deserts? Would our precious land and all the land between the two great rivers just wash away? Would our stony, dusty roads and tracks disappear, together with everything and everyone that was familiar to us? Would we really have to leave our animals and our home behind? It didn't bear thinking about. More and more thoughts and questions flooded our minds as we pictured the future we had ahead of us, and none of our conclusions were particularly pleasant.

"Don't worry, if he is serious about the dimensions of this boat or ark or whatever it's called, it is going to take us so long to build that we will all be dead long before the flood comes anyway," said Japhet.

This thought did nothing to comfort any of us and boat-building on such a huge scale, or indeed on any scale, in preparation for some terrible prediction to come true, certainly wasn't the way I wanted to spend the rest of my life. Up until then I had left things to fate and then just got on with things, but our lives had been normal then. How on earth could everything change so suddenly? Father had turned our world upside down.

As for the animals that we were to take on board, Father told us that when the time came, which would be some way ahead when the ark was nearing completion, we were to choose the finest examples of each species that we could. Unfortunately we would be in competition with the priests, who had always thought that taking the best animals as sacrifices was their prerogative. I could see more problems ahead straight away.

"Not many of ours will make it then," Ham observed bluntly.

At this Japhet looked worried. He was obviously thinking about his dog.

"Oh don't worry Japhet, I'm sure he'll be all right," I told him. "We'll need him to round up all the animals Father talked about." But in my heart, I knew that Dog, an aggressive, snaggle-toothed beast with dark eyes, a permanently fierce expression and unattractive bald patches in his yellow fur, a creature that no one liked except Japhet, was already too old to have any chance of lasting until the ark was built.

It seemed ludicrous to all of us except Father that we embodied the entire workforce for this enormous project. Our mood veered from total disbelief, to hopeless lethargy, to despair and then to a sense of urgency, even rebellion, and back again.

One minute we felt that there was no time to lose and we must start at once, then that we couldn't possibly accomplish such a huge task so it just wasn't worth trying. And, of course, it was still conceivable that Father had actually lost his mind and that this fantastic idea was simply a figment of his insane imagination, which would pose a different worry altogether.

But Father didn't give us much time for doubt to set in or, possibly, a family rebellion; a day or two later he told us that we needed to get started.

Way of Life and Beliefs

As more and more nomadic people began to settle, growing crops around them and domesticating and tending animals for food, they had fewer resources to rely on. Once their lifestyle changed and they no longer moved about looking for different sources of sustenance, they had to survive on the relatively few species of crops they cultivated. If things went wrong and their crops failed to thrive it could be disastrous, a matter of life or death. They needed the conditions to be favourable, with good weather, enough water and crops free of blight or pests to enable them to produce enough food to survive.

People believed that such things were controlled by higher powers and that they needed to propitiate all the appropriate Gods. They made offerings of food or payment to the priests in return for their help in pleasing the Gods who would in turn, they hoped, demonstrate their gratitude by providing the conditions needed for abundant crops.

Consequently, the Mesopotamians were obsessed with predicting the future. For farmers the weather was of paramount importance. For rulers the interpretation of signs could reveal whether to go into battle or not and what the outcome of the battle would be. Success in their interpretations of the future determined whether or not they could maintain their power base and wealth at the pinnacle of their society and provide their subjects with safe and secure lives.

For people to successfully live in close proximity they had to learn to co-operate and more formal codes of social conduct and organisation were needed. Once a family was established in one place it was no longer so easy to simply move away if disagreements arose. Rules evolved to cope with social situations and practical matters such as sanitation, disease, irrigation and food distribution.

Any misfortune was attributed to supernatural forces, which had to be appeased by means of incantations and appropriate offerings. Ghosts were widely believed *in and it was thought that if their needs were not appropriately met they would become vengeful and dangerous.*

The Mesopotamians had a great respect for the past and the lessons to be learned from it, as well as a desire for knowledge of the present and an ability to predict the future. They wanted to make sense of the world that they lived in.

Chapter 3

❖

Once we had reluctantly decided that there was nothing for us to do but to go ahead with Father's plan, we had to decide where we were actually going to build the ark. And it didn't take much foresight to realise that we wouldn't be very popular if we started to build such a huge structure in our own small village, or even nearby. Then it wouldn't have been long before our neighbours stopped laughing and started complaining.

Not surprisingly, news of Father's scheme had spread around the whole area like wildfire, which didn't help. But in spite of our uncertainty and our neighbours' hilarity, there seemed to be no alternative but for the three of us to set out and look for a suitable location to start building. At least our search would get us all away from the village, which had a particular appeal to me as some of our neighbours had started to blame me, as the oldest son of the family, for Father's ideas.

"He's obviously not right in the head."

"It is up to you to placate the Gods, go to the priests and ask them for help."

"Now that your Father is not ... quite himself, you must take over as the head of the family; a steady, wise, young man, just what is needed, you must do something about all this. Your Father and his ideas, you must see he is upsetting our wives and children. Noah must be silenced, and we are all relying on you, Shem."

But although I could see that they had a point and his behaviour was very strange, my loyalty was still to my Father. Could he really have gone mad? Somehow I had a feeling that he hadn't so now it was up to all his family to try and support him and not to plot behind his back.

So where should we look? We needed to be some distance from the village, but in which direction? Out on the plains to the west, south or north? It was a difficult decision. But then Japhet pointed out the obvious, something we had all overlooked. We would need wood to build the ark, and a lot of it, and that meant we had only one choice. We would have to cross the river and go up into the foothills to the east below the tree line, where we could fell enough trees to build the ark.

"But that's so far away," moaned Ham. "It will be all right in the winter when it is cool, but imagine travelling all that way in the heat of the summer."

"Well at least in the summer it will be easy to cross the river bed. In the winter when it is in full flow it will be almost impossible," I pointed out.

"We'll just have to plan," said Japhet. "In the winter ..." And his voice trailed away.

"Anyway it's imperative that we find somewhere surrounded by lots of trees, and the foothills are ideal. I just can't see any alternative."

He was right of course; there was no alternative. When we got to the river, which was very low at this time of year, we simply gathered up our robes when we needed to cross one of the few remaining pools of water and the three of us finally clambered up the pebbly beach on the far side. It was a blazing hot day and once we had crossed the river we set off for the hills with Ham striding out in the lead, his robes flowing round him dramatically. The trek across the plains with no shade was exhausting and Japhet and I were soon trailing far behind him. But at least the heat dried out the lower folds of our robes that had trailed in the river pools.

Up in the hills the heat was still intense even in the shade of the trees. And it wasn't at all easy to find a suitable site; each spot we looked at was either too small, too rocky, had no source of water or was too steep. I began to wonder if we'd ever find anywhere. But after we had tramped about in the blistering heat for several days grumbling and arguing with each other, we finally found a large, flat space, ideally situated just below the tree line, not far from where we had first started looking, that we all agreed on.

"Well thank the Gods," said Ham, throwing his arms in the air in mock praise.

"God," said Japhet.

"Well let's just hope Father thinks it's suitable, too," I said, relieved that we had found somewhere at last. Like all the places we had already looked at, it was covered with plants and grass burned brown and brittle by the sun. There were a fair number of stones and rocks, but none of them terribly large we were relieved to see, as we knew it would be up to us to move them. And what's more, we thought, it was so far away from the village that whatever we did no one could possibly complain that we were making too much noise or getting in their way.

"Well, I can see that it is a good place for getting wood," said Ham, "which is in its favour. But it is also quite a long way from the river and there's only that tiny stream over there to provide water for us, but not enough to float an ark on," and at this he began to laugh hysterically and point at the stream. I wondered briefly if he had sunstroke, but he went on, wiping away tears of laughter: "and from what Father said, with the size of this thing, no lake, pond or even a river is ever going to float it, let alone that piddling little stream."

"Oh do shut up," I snapped, feeling hot and irritable. "I can't think of any way out of all this at the moment. We either build it here with the wood close at hand, or we'll have to drag the wood all the way down to the river."

"Well here it is then," said Ham. "But for goodness sake let us know at once if you do think of any way out of it."

"It is quite a long walk from home," grumbled Japhet, who was always averse to expending any unnecessary energy.

By now I was feeling murderous.

"Well, in my opinion, that's a definite bonus, the further away the better," said Ham, who had finally stopped laughing and flung himself flat out on the ground to rest. "If we've really got to do it, we need it to be far enough away from the village for us to get on with this whole business in peace and quiet. I really don't fancy being the butt of everyone's jokes day after day."

"I suppose you're right," said Japhet, sitting down beside him, "but it's going to be a lot longer than day after day. If Father has the dimensions correct, it'll be more like year after year. To be honest, I can hardly bear to think about it."

"Frankly, I am seriously wondering if Father has gone quite mad," said Ham grimly, "and maybe we should just refuse to go along with it."

"Well don't let him hear you say that," begged Japhet, "or there'll be trouble. I think it would be wise for us to humour him just for now at least and see how it goes."

"Humour him?" Ham bellowed, sitting bolt upright, "humour him? How far do you think we should go to humour him? Build half the ark, or only a quarter? I say we either get on with it and see what happens, or we refuse to start altogether."

"Well I think we had better get on with it for now then," I said. It seemed to be the lesser of two evils.

So, consulting the measurements Father had given us, the three of us roughly paced out the distance we had calculated the base of the ark should cover, end to end and side to side, and fortunately the space we had chosen seemed large enough.

"This is quite ridiculous," said Japhet, cursing as he tripped over a small sapling in his way and then stubbed his toe on a pebble. "Something this size for a couple of camels, cows, chickens and dogs ..." His voice trailed off.

"And sheep, goats, hyenas, vultures, doves, eagles, sparrows, and don't forget probably even snakes and pigs," said Ham, warming to his theme.

"Oh do stop it," begged Japhet. "If things like that have to come on board with us, it just doesn't bear thinking about. I might even volunteer to stay behind myself."

Nonetheless, the following day we asked Father to come with us to show him the spot we had found. Much to our relief, after crossing the bed of the river and tramping up into the foothills with us and then a bit of a search around to find the clearing again, Father said that he thoroughly approved of the prospective location. This was fortunate, as in the heat none of us fancied having to search for another site; in fact, if we'd had to go on looking for another one there was a strong possibility of a revolt.

"Well done you three, this certainly looks as if it should be big enough for the purpose," he said, mopping his brow and surveying the space around him appreciatively before kicking off his sandals and sitting down to rest on a large boulder in the shade.

"Yes it is Father, we measured it out yesterday," I said. "It is big enough for us to build the ark and to have enough space all round it to store materials while we are building."

"Yes, it's ridiculously large isn't it?" muttered Ham who was feeling the heat and sweating profusely.

"I'm sorry Ham, I didn't quite catch that," said Father looking annoyed.

"Father," said Japhet quickly to distract him, "you do realise it is going to be a simply enormous boat? I mean really, really, really large? You don't think that perhaps you might have got some of the measurements wrong?"

Brave man, I thought, waiting for Father's reaction.

"No Japhet, certainly not," he said crossly. "The measurements are correct; there will be a reason why they are as they are. We may not know why yet, but we have been told to build it this size and it is NOT up to us to question God's instructions." I could see his face flush with irritation.

"It looks as if God wants all the animals to have lots and lots of space on board, possibly to imagine they are on a small plain," said Ham, seemingly determined to provoke Father.

Japhet shot a warning glance; it was never wise to make fun of Father, who could be surprisingly touchy, especially when it was hot. Luckily, this time he appeared not to have heard him, perhaps he was too busy mopping his brow for the umpteenth time with a rather damp cloth that he produced from the sleeve of his robe.

33

"Have you noticed the stream, Father?" said Ham.

"Yes, yes, very useful," said Father, "just what we need. I could do with a drink from it right now."

"But do you think it will float the ark?" Ham couldn't resist asking. He seemed really determined to push his luck.

"Ham, it does not have to float the ark, the ark will be floated by the flood, you foolish boy. Don't you ever listen to anything I say?"

"So the flood will come right up here on the hillside?" Ham asked quietly. But Father ignored him.

Where?

The Bible does not tell us exactly where Noah lived with his family before the flood, but it is most likely to have been in an area that produced good crops and fine animals, which would have been made possible by the use of extensive irrigation schemes.

One likely site is the fertile plain of ancient Mesopotamia, lying between the Tigris and Euphrates Rivers (modern-day Iraq) known as the 'Cradle of Civilisation'.

A large amount of food would have been needed for the voyage as well as the finest animals available to breed from in the future. A good supply of wood would also have been needed to build the ark, which was an enormous vessel, even by today's standards.

෴

Chapter 4

❖

Having found a suitable site on which to build the ark, we returned to the village with a gratifying sense of achievement and spent the next few weeks preparing for the huge task ahead. All of us were anxious not to incite any more ridicule from our neighbours than we could help, so we did our best not to attract too much attention and all of us avoided mentioning the ark as much as we could.

Essentially, building the ark was going to be a vast feat of carpentry, so we needed chisels, mallets, cutting saws, twine for binding and carrying and much else besides. We already had quite a good selection of tools, but not nearly enough, so we made some more and bartered with our neighbours for others. We also looked at the small wooden fishing boats and the circular crafts made of woven reeds moored down by the river, carefully examining their construction. We certainly needed all the information we could get to help us build an ark.

Finally it was time to make a start, and it took our donkeys and the mule journey after journey, day after day, with heavily laden pannier baskets to transport everything that we needed up to the building site. At the first river crossing my heart was in my mouth; the beasts were carrying so much that one slip or stumble on the rocks of the river bed and they could have fallen and badly injured themselves. But they seemed to have an unerring instinct for which route to take and all of them reached the other side unscathed. It helped that as the summer went on the heat of the sun largely evaporated even the deepest of the remaining pools in the riverbed. As it was, the effort it took them to carry the panniers of tools up to the site made their coats so dark with sweat that it looked as if they had been submerged on the river crossing anyway. Occasionally, when we had overloaded one of the animals, we had to take its whole load off and re-pack it more lightly in order to get across the river, which meant returning for the rest later, never a popular option.

All of us were dreading the prospect of labouring in such heat, although Father didn't seem to take much account of this; he was just keen to get started. Ham and Japhet did their best to delay things as much as possible by telling him that there was still a lot more we needed to do at home before we were free to work on the ark. But finally our excuses ran out and we couldn't think of any more convincing reasons to put off starting. So, with heavy hearts and a great deal of sweating and grumbling, we began to make the daily journey out to the building site. But in spite of leaving early in the day before the sun was fully up and the heat became unbearable, we found it all exceedingly hard.

The best bit of the journey by far was paddling through any of the shallow pools that were still left in the riverbed on the way there and back. On the way out we had the energy to splash about, but by the end of the day we were so exhausted that we were just glad to wade through the water and cool down a bit before we reached home.

From the very beginning, Father made it clear to all of us that from now on we were to take his instructions seriously and regard building the ark as the most important thing in our lives. At the start of every day he led us in a prayer asking God to bless our work, which was usually enough to start Ham complaining, as he did at the slightest provocation, that he still couldn't understand why we had to build the ark ourselves. Couldn't Father's all-powerful God just provide us with one ready-made?

He hoped in vain.

Accordingly, we spent all our days in the hills round the site cutting down trees, sawing them into a moveable size and then dragging or rolling them down to the clearing where we sawed them into planks. Later on we learned how to soak them in the stream and weigh them down with stones to bend them into curves where necessary. It was hard, tedious work.

As well as this we had to do our best to keep up with our normal daily life as well, providing food and looking after the rest of the family. Somewhat surprisingly, in spite of our exhaustion, we found that working together was unexpectedly satisfying and agreeable, with far less bickering and arguing amongst us than I would ever have believed possible. Maybe we just didn't have the energy for it. Also the enmity of the priests and the mockery our neighbours, which we were constantly subjected to, helped draw us all closer together for protection, trying to make sense of what we were doing.

Once we had actually started work on the ark, our initial doubts about the whole idea seemed to diminish and we gradually came to accept that this really was going to be a huge part of our life for the foreseeable future. It was our reality now, how we spent our days, not just some outlandish scheme that Father had thought up to pass the time, or gain attention. And the harder we worked the fitter we became and consequently the work seemed a bit less exhausting, although none of us could work up much enthusiasm for endlessly sawing planks, which we all found tiring and extremely monotonous.

It was not only our lives that were disrupted by working on the ark. The animals and birds that lived amongst the trees that we were cutting down couldn't have been very happy at being disturbed and, in some unfortunate cases, losing their homes. So Japhet suggested that it would be a good idea to leave some of the trees close to the ark standing, to provide some shelter for everything we had not already driven away with the noise of our sawing and chatter. He pointed out that the roots of the trees around the site held the earth of the hillside together in an underground mesh and cutting down too many trees close to the ark might cause a landslip onto the clearing. We would benefit as well if some of these trees were left standing, as they would provide us with somewhere shady to sit when we were resting. The only disadvantage to this was that they sometimes blocked the route to the clearing when we rolled tree trunks downhill.

Working away from the village for most of the time meant that our wives missed our company and help with the daily chores and they all started to complain that they felt lonely and abandoned. We worked such long hours that they didn't see us at all during the day and, by the time we got home in the evening, we were so exhausted that we could hardly talk and all we wanted to do was sleep. Ham often fell asleep at the table and Japhet frequently nodded off before he had even started his evening meal. So it was decided that it would be better for everyone if Mother and our wives came out to the clearing sometimes to keep us company.

Everyone welcomed this idea except for Nahlat. To Ham's disappointment, she totally refused to leave our home in the village and no amount of persuasion would get her to change her mind. Ham was distraught. "The priests must have put a spell or a curse on her," he said.

"Oh never mind," said Mother. "It will be nothing of the sort and she'll soon get tired of being on her own, just you wait and see."

But it was a long time before Nahlat came out to the clearing. She seemed to enjoy being on her own, left in peace and not being asked to do anything she didn't want to do.

In the meantime Ham grew more and more grumpy, regularly throwing his tools down on the ground in a rage and swearing the most ear-shrivelling oaths. I entreated Salit to try and persuade Nahlat to join us all but to no avail.

Fortunately for the rest of us, at times of the year when the river was low enough to cross safely, the other wives made their way out to the hillside to keep us company and watch us working. They set off much later than we did, as they had all the chores to do at home but they brought our food with them. This made things easier all round and we enjoyed having their company, although in all honesty we were too busy to spend much time with them but at least they were no longer so lonely. Mother didn't always come

39

with them as in the heat of high summer the journey was too long and tiring for her, although we all started to stay up at the clearing overnight sometimes, using some of the off-cuts from the planks to make quite a comfortable shelter.

With so much to do on the site, it was obvious that we could no longer spare Ham or Japhet to go off with our animals for weeks on end as they used to do, but we still needed the milk and the meat the goats and sheep provided.

"I never thought I'd miss doing my turn of sheep-watching," Ham said incredulously. "I actually miss the peace and quiet. Can you believe it?"

So we brought the herd out to graze on the pastures below the ark and paid a lad from the village to tend them for us.

"I don't know who is the more stupid, him or the sheep," said Japhet after watching him critically for a while.

But we didn't have the time to be too concerned and watching some of his antics was entertaining; although the sheep were not known for their intelligence and the goats were wilful and stubborn, they usually managed to outwit him and do whatever they pleased.

"He is useless, let's face it," said Ham bluntly. "All that can be said in his favour is that I suppose he would shout out if there was any real trouble or danger and we could go and sort it out."

"Exactly," said Father. "Now is not the time to worry about the little things in life and what is the alternative?"

With the extra help from our wives at the site, we were able to start growing a few basic crops near the stream so that we all had as much time as possible to labour on the ark. In addition, growing them nearby meant that they didn't need to be transported up from the village once they had been harvested, just stored safely near the ark, ready for use. Mother even brought some of her precious chickens up to the clearing and then we had the benefit of fresh eggs and the homely clucking of hens around us.

Things were settling down into a pleasant routine and I was particularly proud of Salit. As the most practical and easy going of our wives, she was always willing to have a go at any of the extra tasks that needed doing, even some of the heavier work. She had always been unusually good at sharpening our knives at home and whenever there was nothing else to do, she would sit and sharpen the chisels and saws that we used to cut and shape the wood for the ark, cheerfully ignoring any suggestions that it was man's work.

By contrast, when she finally joined us, Ham's wife Nahlat refused to do anything useful at all. She said she missed her family and she complained that she was frightened of animals and that they made her sneeze and smelt horrible. And what's more, we could definitely leave her behind, because she wasn't going to get on the ark, or be involved with the ark in any way, whatever Father said. She seemed to have forgotten how to do any of the things Mother had taught her and she stubbornly refused to try. So, rather than force the issue, it was decided that the best thing to do was to leave her to her own devices until she had come to terms with the situation, or sheer boredom drove her to do something vaguely helpful.

She was a stubborn young woman, so that took quite a long time.

Before all this, Japhet's wife Arisisah had been like a little mouse, timid and unsure, but now she was an invaluable help to us all, ready to try anything. When there was nothing else for her to do, she and Mother would sit making tallow candles out of animal fat, or mending our torn and worn clothes, while Nahlat looked on disinterestedly, a look she had honed to perfection.

As far as I can recall, the most exciting thing that ever happened in our village before Father and his ark was the arrival of the odd soothsayer or travelling storyteller or pedlar who, if we were lucky, might also attempt the odd trick or two to amuse and confound us. With so little other entertainment for the villagers, it was hardly surprising that the stories of our efforts with the ark continued to entertain everyone.

If we had merely been trying to build a small fishing boat, it would have kept all the old men and women in the village amused for ages, watching and commenting as they always did about anything at all out of the ordinary. But to attempt to build something the size of the ark was regarded as an enterprise so mad that usually the mere mention of the word 'ark' was enough to set them all off, cackling with mirth and making fun of us.

"I always wanted to be the laughing stock of the entire village," said Ham crossly and I had to agree with him. It was very hard to put up with at times.

Much later on, when visitors could see the overall shape of the ark beginning to appear and its proportions became easier to visualise, we were taken slightly more seriously and then they couldn't wait to get back to the village to tell everyone else about it. This renewed interest meant that more and more people started to come out to watch our progress. After the long walk up to the clearing most of them would make a day of their visit, settling down in the shade to eat the food that they had brought with them, while they watched us labouring away in front of them for entertainment.

Some months after we had permanently moved out of the village and up to the clearing, Arisisah's family came out to the site to try and persuade her to leave Japhet, son of the 'Mad Noah' and return home with them. Home was of course a tent on the surrounding plains as they were nomadic shepherds. But by now Arisisah and Japhet were more in love than ever and no amount of coaxing and cajoling would make her contemplate leaving him. However, the whole episode was extremely distressing for both her and her family; many tears were shed and angry words exchanged on both sides. Their visit was a disaster and greatly upset all of us.

Fortunately, Salit's family were far more pragmatic about the whole affair and we heard nothing at all from Nahlat's family; they probably didn't want to risk having to return her dowry and they did have five other daughters after all. I can remember thinking that if any of the other sisters were even half as awkward as Nahlat could be, the remaining five would definitely be enough to be going on with.

Although looking back I seem to remember mostly the weather as terrifically hot, there must have been almost as many times when it was cold or we had to work in torrential rain. I also remember how irritated we got when none of the other men who came out to watch us building the ark ever made any attempt to help us. Not even when they could see that we were struggling to do something, right in front of them. Nor were they above shouting sarcastically helpful remarks and directions to us, while they themselves did nothing but laze in the shade. Father and Japhet were usually so engrossed in what they were doing that they took no notice, but Ham and I found it very hard not to react angrily. I couldn't help remembering all the times in the past when we had helped them.

"Oh they just don't understand," was all Father said, mildly. "And, sadly for them, I don't think they ever will now, or not until it is too late."

As the weeks turned into months and the months turned into many long years, we were no longer the focus of much curiosity and our value as the local entertainment was usurped by other things, such as a sheep that had an improbably large number of lambs, or maybe it was legs, odd things like that ... I don't recall exactly what now. So once most of the village had tramped up to see the ark site a few times and noted our slow progress, they grew bored and left us in peace. A few strangers still turned up every now and then, though, to see if what they had heard on their travels was actually true.

"If I had a sheep for every time I heard some fool say 'Well it doesn't look much like a boat to me', I'd have the largest flock in the land by now," grumbled Ham.

One of the greatest benefits of being left alone out on the hillside was that in the terrific heat we often had to endure, we could strip off and work in just our under-garments, which made life a lot more bearable. Of course when our wives were there, we had to be

43

careful of our behaviour and do nothing to make them feel embarrassed. Unlike them we were also able to cool off by splashing about in the stream, something we hadn't done since we were children and it became one of the few highlights of our day. Sometimes I felt sorry for our wives, whose only real respite from the heat was to sit in the shade, or have a careful paddle, no higher than their knees, or let their robes trail in the stream to cool them, when they went to collect our drinking water. Although Salit did admit to me years later, that when all the men had left the site to cut down trees or whatever, the women took the opportunity to splash about as vigorously as we did and submerged themselves in the stream, which I was glad to hear.

Progress was depressingly slow at times. Even after all our years of hard work and preparation, endlessly cutting down swathes of trees for planks and joists, the huge dimensions of the ark seemed to dwarf all our efforts and it was still little more than a skeleton. The edges of the clearing were covered with huge piles of planks and the small stream running past us down to the river was full of yet more planks lying side by side. These were weighed down with stones in the centre to give them the necessary curve we needed for the prow and the stern of the ark. But by now, if you had a good imagination, you could see that the ark's basic shape was slowly beginning to emerge; its outline was delineated by enormous wooden struts supporting huge joists, which stretched nearly the whole length of the clearing. However, the vast overall size of the ark meant that the struts were so far apart that it was still hard for anyone outside the family to visualise what the ark might finally look like and even we didn't find it that easy.

By now the clearing looked like a giant wood yard, with piles and piles of planks that we had laboriously sawn and stacked by size and shape, ready to be fastened into place. We had learned from bitter experience the benefits of being methodical. To begin with the freshly cut planks oozed sweet-smelling resin, which made them sticky and awkward to handle. But as the wood weathered over time its exterior turned grey and brittle and part of

44

every day was spent agonising over splinters of wood in our hands and other body parts. Fortunately Arisisah became an expert at extracting these for us as painlessly as possible.

On the whole the few visitors that still appeared were disappointed with what they saw; we could see it in their faces. After all this time, our progress was painfully slow and they didn't know or care that each of the enormous supporting struts was the result of weeks or even months of our hard labour, sawing, dragging and fixing them in place. So it wasn't really surprising that they were bemused or unimpressed. There were times when we ourselves looked around the wood-strewn site and wondered what on earth we were doing.

We worked so hard during the day and were usually quite far apart, so we had very few opportunities to talk to each other. Very often we didn't even have our breaks at the same time. But now and then Father would call us together and we would all down tools. Maybe he thought such meetings would inspire us or reignite our enthusiasm, which to be honest had never been that great. The last time we had listened, unmoved, while he told us there were to be three interior decks and the final height of the whole ark was going to be higher than the tallest tree. Of course we already knew its length and width, which by now took up most of the clearing, but we had not given much thought to what the interior would be like and to be honest we hadn't the time or the energy. So when we heard these plans, far from being inspired, our main concern was what an enormous amount of work we still had to complete before the ark would be finished.

Documentation

How do we know about the people that lived in Mesopotamia so long ago? The first written records found were in Babylonian cuneiform script, inscribed on clay tablets. Inscribing on these clay tablets was a method of keeping records that was already in use in that area at least 1,000 years before the estimated date of the flood. Originally it was only used for practical administration and to make lists, record items and amounts of goods, crops and building materials. For these purposes a system using pictograms was adequate. Only later were symbols developed which enabled scribes to write down stories and record historical events. These symbols increased in number and complexity as people wished to record feelings, thoughts and more complex and nuanced ideas. And slowly the written word became the most important way of recording events and information, taking over from word-of-mouth.

Following the use of cuneiform script on clay tablets, long texts and stories started to be written down on scrolls of papyrus or parchment with reed pens, using ink made of soot, water and gum.

From ancient times, the location of Mesopotamia as a crossroads led to a population created by a fusion of many different peoples. And the sophistication of the Sumerian people, the first major civilisation to live in this area of southern Mesopotamia, led to it being known as the 'Cradle of Civilisation'.

☙❧

Chapter 5

❦

There came a day when nothing seemed to be going right for any of us and our morale was at rock bottom. The sun blazed down so fiercely that even in the shade the heat was almost unbearable and the sheer enormity of the task of building the ark seemed overwhelming and futile. Our efforts seemed to be getting us nowhere and everything we were trying to do was hard going. Time seemed to be going backwards and although it felt as if we had been working for hours it still wasn't anywhere near midday.

Already Japhet and I seemed to have got more splinters in our hands during one morning than we normally got in a week and Ham kept hitting his fingers with his mallet, which was a sure sign that he was tired and his attention was wandering. The air was blue with his curses and he was flinging his tools all over the clearing.

Then, three strangers arrived.

I don't think we even noticed them at first; they stood there so quietly. And although there was nothing particularly unusual about them, neither was there anything familiar. Even now looking back, it is hard to explain exactly why, but they were unlike anyone else we had ever seen. Nothing about them gave us any indication as to where they had come from or why they were here. It was not as if we were unused to visits from inquisitive strangers – we had seen plenty of them – but there was just something about these three and it was hard to put our finger on exactly what it was.

"Just come to laze about and watch us sweat, like everyone else I expect," said Japhet with good reason, for that's what usually happened.

All the same, we were glad for the break in the tedium that their arrival caused and it was a good excuse to down tools for a while. But I sensed that for some reason, Father was worried by their appearance; perhaps he thought they had come to cause trouble of some kind.

All three of them were tall, fine-looking men with fairer skin than was usual in these parts and they all wore similar robes, of a kind that were commonly worn by travellers. However, there was one very unusual thing about them; they seemed to have few if any belongings with them and they had no donkey or pack animal to carry anything for them either.

They didn't come over the clearing to see us straight away but, having raised their hands in greeting, they settled down in the shade of the remaining trees on the south side of the clearing to rest for a while.

"There, what did I tell you?" said Japhet. "Sightseers."

But before long, one of them rose to his feet and walked over to Father to make polite greetings. Then to our absolute amazement, we heard him ask Father if there was anything useful they could do to help? Ham, who was working nearby, nearly fell off his ladder with surprise. In all the years that we had worked on the ark, not one single person outside our family had ever offered to help us. Father looked a little doubtful, but when he saw Ham's expression of hopeful anticipation willing him to say yes, he finally smiled and gratefully accepted the offer.

Japhet, who was in charge of the order of work on the ark, lost no time in telling the three of them what we most needed help with. And to his relief, they got straight on with what he had suggested without arguing. In fact they seemed to be such competent workers that when we were all discussing them later on, we thought it was quite likely that they were itinerant builders or carpenters.

Our wives had been watching them with great interest as well, trying to guess where they came from and who they were. But, like us, they could not see anything about the three men that marked them out or helped to identify them in any way. We would just have to wait until they told us more about themselves.

Salit had heard one of them introduce himself to Father as Kafzeil, which wasn't a local name, and the other two men were called Samael and Anael. And amazingly, in all the time that they were with us, we never really found out anything else about them. Not that they were unfriendly, there was just a kind of reserve in their manner that made us feel that somehow it wouldn't have been right to question them and they never volunteered any information about themselves. In fact, looking back now, it seems a far odder situation than we actually found it back then. We were so grateful to have their help that we didn't really worry about the details and we certainly didn't want to upset them by asking intrusive questions.

From the very first day the three of them worked steadily and efficiently, fitting in extraordinarily well and keeping pace with us with no trouble at all. They had a particularly steadying effect on Ham, who was normally a fast and sometimes slapdash worker, regularly hitting his fingers or thumbs with his mallet and swearing colourful oaths, which made Father wince if he was within earshot. But somehow the presence of these men seemed to have a calming effect on him and he began to slow down and work to their rhythm, something that all Father's previous efforts had never managed to achieve. So, in their quiet and unobtrusive way, they seemed to bring a kind of order to the clearing, something that had been missing before, amongst the piles of planks and mountains of sawdust.

From the very start it was obvious that with a workforce of seven we were going to make a lot more progress than we had been able to make with only four of us. So within hours of the strangers joining us, I was not surprised when I saw Father go a little way up the hill above us and drop to his knees in prayer. And although he usually did this in private, this time he didn't seem to mind who saw him thanking God for the help that had come so unexpectedly, just when we needed it the most.

And to our great relief the men showed no signs of wanting to go on their way the next day or indeed any of the following ones.

"If they leave us now, I definitely think I'll go with them," Ham said. "In some strange way, their being here makes all this a bit more bearable."

"A lot more bearable," added Japhet.

"I agree," I said.

So weeks and then months passed and nothing was ever said about how long they would stay, or when they would leave. We certainly didn't want to put the idea in their heads by asking them, so that was another thing we never mentioned. They worked steadily all day, often starting before the rest of us and in the evening after we had all eaten they seemed quite happy to camp down by the stream close to the ark. They never showed any interest in visiting the village with us or of wanting to go much further afield than the woods around the clearing and the surrounding hills.

Early one morning, not that long after the strangers arrived, Japhet was walking up the hill with his dog when he happened to look down on the proceedings in the clearing. Suddenly he started to shout, "Father! Father?" And he ran back down the hill at break-neck speed, almost tripping over his excited dog that was barking and leaping round him, to where Father was sitting in the shade quietly chiselling out dowel holes in the planks.

"Father!" he puffed, as the extra exertion had taken his breath away.

"What is it my son?" asked Father calmly, looking up at his red-faced son.

"It's a disaster Father, a DISASTER and I can't believe that I've only just noticed. I'm so sorry, the shape... looking at the shape of the ark... it is odd. You know I have always had my doubts about it, but this," he panted, "this is terrible. All this time and no one noticed... I never noticed."

"Noticed what?" asked Father, remaining calm.

"We have no rudder and we have no plan to put a rudder on the ark. So how are we going to steer?" Japhet shouted rather hysterically, in spite of being so close to Father, who drew back from him in alarm.

50

"I know that Japhet, of course I know, but I also know that it's not a problem."

"Not a problem? Of course it's a problem, it must be a problem, how are we going to steer, then?" yelled Japhet, almost hysterical. "All boats have to be steered; even I know that boats have to be steered. Oh, how could I have let this happen?" he wailed. "And what will the others say? It's my responsibility to notice such things. It's all my fault."

He was so busy blaming himself that he had not taken in what Father said.

"Japhet, I'm telling you that it's all right, we don't need a rudder," said Father quietly, putting his hand on Japhet's arm to calm him down.

Anael was working close by and couldn't help hearing the commotion. Japhet looked desperately to him for his reaction, but he merely gave the slightest of nods, as if to confirm what Father had said.

"God will guide us on the voyage," said Father in a tone of authority that suggested further discussion was out of the question and so the matter was dropped.

Having three extra workers had made a huge difference and our increased work rate pushed things along noticeably faster. We were making progress at last. And it wasn't long before the ark really started to take shape and look like a boat, rather than an enormous pile of planks in a vast wood yard. Once word of this got back to our old neighbours some of them began to take an interest in us again and travel out to the foothills to see for themselves. By now, even the most sceptical of them had to admit that the shape of the ark was becoming more obvious and they were frankly awestruck. And although I hate to admit it, we all found this rather encouraging. Once we started to fix the first planks to the joists – "fleshing out the bones," as Father put it – it finally began to look like the huge vessel that it was always meant to be.

The resurgence of interest in the ark was such that it even lured some of the local fishermen away from their livelihood on the rivers and up into the hills for the first time, to see for themselves what was going on. But despite being astonished by the sheer size of the ark, they were very critical of the design. They immediately noticed that there was no rudder and were also quick to point out that we didn't appear to have made a mast for the sail, either. To be honest, it did seem to have evolved into a rather unconventional shape. And as they wandered around the clearing looking at the ark from various angles their suspicions were confirmed: it just didn't seem right somehow, and they weren't afraid to say so.

As luck would have it, they almost unerringly chose Ham to discuss this with and predictably a row would ensue. His furious retorts to their suggestions merely reinforced their view that not only Father, but the rest of his family too were still totally and utterly mad. And the size of it... unbelievable. How could any sane man think that something so vast and so far from a large river or the sea would ever float, or indeed ever get finished? I had doubts about this myself, which were reinforced when I heard them voiced by others. All of us felt anxious, except for Father of course, and maybe even he did sometimes, in the dark watches of the night.

Even at this late stage, Father had not entirely given up trying to warn anyone he came across of the perils to come if they did not mend their ways, warning them yet again about the terrible flood that would be the consequence of God's wrath if they did not. But even watching us build this amazing ark to withstand the effects of the terrifying flood that Father was predicting didn't make any difference and still no one believed him. Their minds were made up and they utterly refused to take our efforts or Father's warnings seriously. As one of them said to me, "You don't really believe all this do you, Shem? Why should 'God' choose to save your family? You lot, you're no angels, come on, be honest. You're no better than the rest of us and you're mad as well."

So our neighbours and all the other local people carried on as usual, ignoring Father and continuing to make offerings to the different Gods of the harvest and the herds and the Gods of the sun and all the rest of them, as they had done for generations, taking the advice of the priests as they always had done and no notice of Father's warnings of impending doom. And, in all honesty, it did seem as if the Gods appreciated all their gifts and offerings. The weather was getting even better and their crops and animals continued to flourish. Of course this only served to reinforce their view that Father and his bizarre predictions, to say nothing of his three compliant sons, their wives and their three deluded friends really were quite mad.

"Have you ever thought what it would mean if everyone did suddenly start to take notice of Father?" said Ham. "If everyone obeyed the word of God, there'd be no need of a flood and we'd have spent all these years breaking our backs to build the ark for nothing. I've a good mind to tell him to shut up with his warnings from now on, just in case they all start to believe him and start to change their ways."

"I don't think you've got anything to worry about," said Japhet. "So far, have you heard even one person outside the family take what he says seriously?"

"Well I did see him make some little children cry with fright once," said Ham. "But their parents soon cheered them up by telling them Father was a crazy man and there was no need to take any notice of what he said."

"I think you can relax then," said Japhet, "No one is going to change their mind now. Extraordinary really, not one person has. It makes you think, doesn't it?"

"Oh let's just get on with it," I said.

Still there was no disputing the fact that so far absolutely nothing had happened to indicate God's displeasure, except for the message that Father had received. So I suppose the people thought, not unreasonably, such good weather, fine crops and healthy animals were a very odd way indeed for God to show his displeasure with the people on earth. And how was it compatible with Noah's warnings that God wanted them all to mend their ways, if he continued to shower them with good fortune?

It was hard not to wonder why, if God was so displeased with them, he didn't demonstrate his displeasure by giving them a drought maybe, a plague of locusts, crop blight, something to convince them Father was right. Until they had some kind of sign that they could understand, they would see no good reason to change. They clearly didn't consider watching a mad old man and his crazy family spend years and years building a huge boat in the foothills a sign worth taking note of.

"To be honest Father," Japhet said one day when he was feeling brave, "I do think they have a point. Things really are going well for everybody."

"I agree," Ham chipped in.

But before he could continue Father stopped him, raising his hand for silence.

"My sons, just think, with what we have got before us we will need a vast quantity of supplies and fine animals. Just how do you imagine we will be able to get together all that will be required without good conditions? You are all farmers and you should know that. If we had droughts and bad harvests, where would we get our stores of food for the voyage, to feed all the fine animals that we need to breed from?"

What Father had said was undeniably right and a slight chill went through us all on hearing this logic. So once more we set to building the ark, following Father's instructions. And during all those long and arduous years the only people that ever gave us any help were the three strangers who worked alongside us in all weathers.

Possible Sources

Some historians and theologians believe the story of Noah is simply a version of the ancient Mesopotamian story of King Gilgamesh, who embarked on an eventful journey in search of immortality, which was ultimately denied him by the gods. However, somewhat problematically for this theory, there are several different versions of the story and not all of them include a flood.

The story of Gilgamesh, the legendary King of Uruk, was one of the first and longest stories ever to be transcribed on cuneiform tablets over 1,000 years before the Old Testament of the Bible was written down. By then, symbols had been developed for movement, characters and action, which enabled stories to be more permanently recorded by writing them down. Thus, they were less likely to be forgotten or distorted in the verbal repetition of them.

Many countries all over the world, from the Americas to Asia, have a story of a great flood as part of their heritage, but it has proved virtually impossible to tie them all together geologically or historically in order to prove incontrovertibly that there was one worldwide flood.

☙❧

Chapter 6

❦

After all our work and with the completion of the ark finally in sight, there were still no signs whatsoever of any major change in the weather. In the winter it was still temperate with just the right amount of rain for the crops and in the summer the sky was blue with no clouds to be seen. Everything flourished, there was plenty of food for us all, our animals were well covered, neither fat nor thin, in an ideal condition to provide good strong breeding stock. And when it rained it never showed any signs whatsoever of turning into Father's flood. But now we could see the logic of these perfect conditions, namely to provide us with adequate provisions and strong, fit animals, working hard to finish the ark made much more sense to us.

Finally, after many long years of arduous work the ark was nearly complete and we stayed up in the hills on site most of the time, only occasionally returning to the village, which was never a very pleasant experience. Over the years the mockery of our neighbours had hardened into real antipathy, which had been enthusiastically fostered and encouraged by the priests. If any of us had to go to the village for any reason, we couldn't wait to leave again and return to the shelter of the clearing and the family.

"I feel as if they all really hate us now," said Japhet. "I never thought I'd live to say it, but if I never had to go there again, I wouldn't mind. I just don't feel safe there anymore." The rest of us knew exactly what he meant; we all felt the same.

For a long time now our animals had lived around us, feeding on the plants that still grew abundantly in the clearing nearby or out on the plain below the tree line, while the hardier ones scrambled about on the hillside above. Whenever there was a brief lull in the sawing and banging, we could hear the gentler sounds of grazing animals relentlessly pulling and crunching on the nearby vegetation. Our own diet was almost unchanged; we ate what we'd always eaten: fruit, plants and cereals with some meat and occasionally fish, together with milk from the sheep and goats and, of course, beer and wine.

Looking back, the worst time of all without a doubt was at the very start when we spent nearly all of our time felling an enormous number of trees, which we then laboriously cut into planks and joists. Even now, it makes me ache to remember just how exhausting and tedious it was, day after day, month after month, year after year, to say nothing of the painful calluses we all had on our hands. And I remember how lonely we felt sometimes. All our village friends and acquaintances had, without exception, written us off as crazy and deserted us long ago. So for weeks on end there was no one to talk to but the other members of the family and even that could be difficult as during the day it was usually too noisy to hear each other and at night we were just too tired. And as we were all doing pretty much the same thing day in day out, the topics for stimulating conversation were limited.

And of course we lived with the knowledge that everyone else we knew was going about their lives as usual; it was certainly true of our old neighbours who seemed to be living the good life, celebrating their excellent crops and continuing to make offerings to thank the Gods for their bounty. And as far as we knew all the animals, birds and reptiles continued to live in relative harmony as well. In our ignorance we had absolutely no idea of the number and variety of the animals we would need to house on the ark – how could we have? We had no idea how many exotic species there would be either, because with our limited experience we had never seen or even heard about most of them or anything like them before. Our knowledge was limited to quite a small number of familiar animals, certainly not any creatures so strange that we couldn't have imagined them in our wildest dreams, or most horrific nightmares.

All that was still to come.

But by now, quite unknown to us, strange things were beginning to happen all around us and in far away places that we had no knowledge of. Far and wide, animals and birds of every conceivable kind were getting strangely restless. The bravest and strongest of these beasts had begun to feel unsettled, with an irresistible urge to move on, abandoning the rest of their kind and leaving their familiar surroundings, to set off for the unknown in the direction of the ark. Out on the plains, for instance, one or more pairs of the strongest animals, male and female, would separate from the rest of the herd and drive the others back if they tried to follow. Sometimes only one of the pairs would be tough enough to complete a particularly long journey and the weaker ones would fall by the wayside.

Solitary animals were drawn in our direction as well. These were species where the male and female tended to live separately, but as they got nearer to the ark they paired up so that they usually arrived together. Day by day and little by little, they all moved closer to the ark.

And however far away they were when they started their journey, the destination they were drawn towards from every direction, near and far, was the same: the ark, which seemed to exert some kind of a magnetic pull on them.

All this time we were working long hard hours and so were our wives, even Nahlat, who had finally got over her rebellious period and was as helpful and willing as anyone else. While we worked on the last stages of the building, they were vital in helping us to obtain the supplies that we were going to need if we were to live on the ark. Our neighbours, who didn't have the distraction of having to build an enormous ark, had excelled themselves by growing huge quantities of surplus food, so much in fact that they didn't really know what to do with it. And our wives' bargaining and bartering skills were astonishing; Salit and Arisisah were particularly tough negotiators. Father had told them to barter absolutely everything we wouldn't need on the ark, which seemed

58

to be most of our possessions in his opinion. So as our neighbours really had no alternative market and no idea what else to do with it, we were able to assemble the massive amount of food and provisions that Father assured us would be needed to feed everyone on extremely reasonable terms. This did not endear us to our neighbours or the local farmers, with whom we were already hugely unpopular. Of course, once all this food was brought to the clearing, we couldn't just leave it to be eaten by all the loose animals that were roaming about. We had to store it in an orderly way. More hard work, I thought glumly.

"Well I'll be damned if we ask anyone else to help us," said Ham. "We've provided quite enough amusement for our neighbours already and we don't seem to have any friends left amongst them, so we'll do it by ourselves."

This was undoubtedly true, so the rest of us reluctantly agreed with him that we had to press on alone and forget about getting anyone else to join us.

Nothing could have been quite as daunting as actually building the ark from scratch, so any change of routine, even one that involved more hard work, was welcome. Suddenly, we were surrounded by mountains of food and our wives made the most of this opportunity to make particularly nourishing and delicious meals for us all which, as you can imagine, was a very welcome state of affairs. Working on the ark had taken up most of our time and we had had years of barely producing enough food for us all to survive on.

It was far more difficult to persuade the farmers to part with their finest animals to take on the ark. They drove a far harder bargain over livestock, which they were extremely unwilling to part with. And there were further complications with the priests, who also had their eyes on the same fine animals for sacrificial purposes. But in the end, because at least we gave them something and the priests gave them nothing, we were able to tempt most of them into parting with some of their finest animals in exchange for almost all of our sheep, goats and chickens.

Once we had started negotiations, it wasn't long before most of our flock had gone and so had nearly all our chickens and dogs. By now, Japhet's faithful old hound had been dead for years and so was our one ancient camel, a rather more malleable creature than Nahlat's dowry camel. In return, all we were left with were seven sheep, seven goats and seven of various other specified animals, together with a few other domestic creatures, that all wandered rather mournfully round the ark clearing, foraging for food. Admittedly our newly acquired stock were very fine beasts but, on the other hand, there were very few of them and it seemed to be a poor bargain in my opinion. It reminded me of the situation after Father had made Nahlat's wedding payment, but a lot worse. Father however seemed pleased with the result and reassured us by saying that it was quality not quantity that mattered now, so we tried our best not to mind either. Ham had suggested that it might be a good idea to tether them in case they suddenly decided to return to their old owners in the village. But Father said it wouldn't be necessary, they would be better left free to forage for as much food as possible before entering the ark and, fortunately, he was right.

The next task was to find pairs of animals that we knew existed but that neither we, nor our neighbours, owned. The three strangers seemed to be very knowledgeable on this score, which was a help and they described a number of animals that we had only heard rumour of and others that we had no idea existed.

Ham saw his chance here. He was absolutely desperate for a change of scene and he managed to persuade Father to let him go off in search of the finest pair of camels and horses that he could find. Father had to agree to this, as the only camels in the village weren't impressive specimens and we knew of no one in the area who owned any horses. To this end, Father gave him nearly all the savings and personal treasures we had not already handed over in our bargaining and bartering, which didn't please Mother very much.

Much later on, when it was too late to do anything about it, we found out that Nahlat had managed to hoard rather more than her fair share of treasures and adornments of gold, deep blue lapis and rich brown cornelian stones, which had been part of her dowry, and hidden them on board. But frankly they didn't really fit in with a life of cooking and animal husbandry, so she didn't have a chance to wear them and after an initial show of outrage by the rest of us, the men forgot all about it, although I am not so sure that the other women did.

So in return for our animals and almost everything else of any value that the eight of us owned, we obtained huge amounts of grain, dried grasses, living trees, vines and seeds, which we needed for the birds and to sow on our future land, also vats of cheese, oil and honey and baskets of dried figs, pomegranates and other fruits, all of which we had to stagger on board with and stow neatly away. We also bartered dried fish from the river fishermen and as much meat as was practicable, which we salted down and stored with the other preserved food. When he saw the finished result, Ham rudely commented that he'd seen more appetising leather sandals. He also observed that with all the extra weight of the supplies on board, it was even more unlikely that the ark would ever float.

The only animals we kept right until the very end were our last donkeys and the mule; they had worked tirelessly for so long now, carrying supplies for us up from the village to the ark, that we felt we couldn't just get rid of them. I was particularly fond of our old mule, which was a lot more placid than some of his predecessors but, as mules don't breed, I had to accept that he would not be coming with us. So in return for years of gruelling hard work trekking backwards and forwards from the village and finally helping us to transport supplies on board, we turned him loose near the ark with the donkeys. It seemed only fair that they should spend their last days with us, if indeed that is what they turned out to be, grazing peacefully amongst the animals that we planned to take onto the ark. I had no heart for bartering them and allowing them to be worked into the ground by strangers.

Meanwhile, as we were making all the final preparations, the skies remained clear and there was still no sign of rain. In fact, it was so dry that the latest crops to be harvested were beginning to suffer from what could almost be called a drought.

Our work on the ark was nearly finished. There was just one small area left which had to be to be waterproofed with boiling pitch resin, which we applied with rag bundles tied to the end of long poles. There was quite a knack to this and anyone who inadvertently flicked specks of hot pitch about was very unpopular indeed with the rest of us. Unlike Ham, I liked the smell of pitch; it was somehow comforting and homely, especially when things got pretty bad as they did on several occasions before we had even boarded the ark.

A particularly low spot occurred when Mother found out that Father had given our house away. I had never seen her that angry before.

"Our house? Are you crazy? Not selling it, not bartering it … giving it away? What are you thinking of, Husband?"

"I could not sell anyone a house when I knew it would soon be under water. The house will not last, I could not cheat my neighbours like that and we will never use it again," said Father. "We have all we need here now anyway."

"Well you know very well they'd think nothing of cheating you. And they don't even believe it is going to be flooded," Mother retorted furiously. "To be frank with you, I have my doubts too, just look at the weather Husband, look at it!" and she dramatically threw her arms wide to encompass the sunny clearing.

But Father merely looked at her reproachfully and gave her a look that even Mother dared not ignore. So that was that.

With the outside of the ark virtually finished, there was still a fair amount of work to do on the inside. Most importantly, we had to finish making the last of the partitions that were needed to keep the various animals separate and safe. We also had to finish putting up the internal gangplanks, which would be used by the smaller animals to get up to the middle deck where they were to be housed. Our living quarters were to be on the middle deck as well, out of the way of the largest of the animals.

While all the animals were to be on the middle or lower decks, the birds were to live above us, on long perching poles traversing the top of the ark below the roof. The whole of the middle deck was to be covered over with plaited reed roofing to protect us from their droppings. This plaited roofing was one of the few things Nahlat actually seemed to enjoy making; there was certainly motivation enough for her to do a thorough job.

The enclosures inside the ark varied from enormous to minute. We divided the spaces up as well as we could to suit all the creatures that we knew about and those that the strangers had told us about.

"Don't worry about it too much, we can always make adjustments later on if we need to," said Father.

At which Ham rolled his eyes in despair.

As far as possible, we tried to think of ways to make the various animals feel at home on the ark. Some stalls were covered with straw, some had branches, some sawdust, of which we had plenty, of course, and some had piles of stones. Naturally we had to carry all this on board and it was exhausting, messy work. The floor was criss-crossed with trickles of earth and sawdust and paths of leaves, twigs and pebbles that we had dropped underfoot on our way to the various enclosures. However, when we had time to stop and look around at what we had achieved, we all agreed that the ark looked very impressive, both inside and out.

"Fit for purpose at last!" Father shouted enthusiastically as he surveyed the final results of so many years' work, then he hugged everyone and clapped us all on the back.

Once the ark had been entirely enclosed and the roof built, most of the natural light was excluded. So, for the last stages of the construction, we had to illuminate the interior both day and night with numerous oil lamps to provide enough light to work by. The flickering flames showed up the wooden planks of the vast interior, streaked orange with wood sap and pitch that shone in the light of the candles where it had collected in the cracks. The supporting beams rose high above us, like the ribs of a colossal animal, and the upper decks extended out from the sides, supported by massive joists made from whole tree trunks. We had kept the vast central space empty, except for some large enclosures and the gangways, water channels and feeding chutes that went up and down the ark from top to bottom. The whole interior smelled strongly of pitch and wood, mingled with the smell of hay and other aromatic supplies that we had stored on board in preparation for the journey, and was not unpleasant.

But while the animals were as well catered for as we could manage, our own living quarters on the mezzanine floor still looked rather bare and uninviting. This had been one of Japhet's main projects, and we had the basics but not much more. There was a large central table surrounded by wide rudimentary seats that we planned to sleep on and shelves with holes carved out of them to fit storage jars and bowls to keep them safe from sliding off and crashing to the floor. Mother rather tactlessly pointed out that it looked a bit bleak and whilst privately I agreed with her I kept it to myself. It wasn't very homely and the animals' comfort seemed to have been taken into account rather more than our own.

Ham, as blunt as ever, said words failed him when he first saw it.

"That will be a first," Japhet retorted crossly.

"Now, now, you can soon put that right, when you have the time," said Father holding up his hand to forestall the start of an argument and keep the peace. "Salit, Nahlat and Arisisah can make things look comfortable and homely in no time. I have every confidence."

I hoped he was right.

To a certain extent he was right, but so many of our belongings had been bartered away for food and animals that our quarters remained plain and serviceable rather than homely.

In spite of Father's conviction, when we looked admiringly at the towering shape of the ark, propped up in the clearing and

looking totally out of place up here on the hillside, it was impossible to imagine there could ever be enough water to float this huge
structure off dry land. No river that we had ever seen was
anything like large enough, not even the great Eastern River beside
our village, which rose dramatically during the spring and winter
rains. For now the nearest water to the ark was a small stream and
we were nowhere near the sea, something that none of us had ever
actually seen. It was hard not to have a nagging feeling that we
might just have finished building and equipping the biggest folly
the world had ever seen.

Animals

God's instructions to Noah about which animals and birds were to be taken on board the ark are clearly laid out in the book of Genesis 6: 19–22.

"And of every living thing, of all flesh, you shall bring two of every kind into the ark, to keep them alive with you; they shall be male and female. Of the birds, according to their kinds, and of the animals according to their kinds, of every creeping thing of the ground according to its kind, two of every kind shall come in to you, to keep them alive. Also take with you every kind of food that is eaten, and store it up; and it shall serve as food for you and for them."

God further instructs Noah in Genesis 7.

"Take with you seven pairs of all clean animals, the male and its mate, and a pair of the animals that are not clean, the male and its mate."

꧁꧂

Chapter 7

❖

During the final stages of preparation, something so strange happened that it finally convinced us that things were going to turn out just as Father had predicted.

Slowly, from every direction, a strange assortment of animals began to arrive around the clearing. They didn't come all that close to the ark at first, as they were timid and nervous of us. But once they had come near enough to see the ark, they never wandered very far away. Some of them we could recognise and identify, but many more were quite unlike anything we had ever seen before. And there were an astonishing number of them; we had absolutely no idea what most of them were, or from where on earth they had arrived.

There were large hairy ones, smooth ones, scaly ones, some had large horns, some small, and they varied in colour from deepest black to brightest white and almost every colour in between. Some stayed down by the river, while others made for the remains of the woods above the ark and yet more settled on the plateau where our sheep and goats had once grazed. And as more and more of them arrived, the stranger they seemed to be. There were armadillos, like giant woodlice, which could roll up in a ball if they were scared, hedgehogs, tiny, dark-eyed and covered with prickles, long-necked giraffes, kangaroos, huge grey elephants, black bears, white bears and vividly coloured birds. We were constantly astonished by the appearance of the new arrivals.

"I am sure that there are more than two of each of them, Father," Japhet pointed out, ever the practical member of the family. "Can that be right?"

But Father didn't answer, so he probably didn't know himself and all we could do was marvel at the variety, quantity and beauty of the beasts as they arrived in the clearing. Even Japhet, who knew much more about a lot of things than the rest of us, said he could never have imagined some of them in his wildest dreams.

"Did you see the ones with necks as long as trees and tiny heads?" I asked him.

"Oh, do stop exaggerating," he replied

"And did you see the ones like black and white striped horses?" asked Ham.

"Oh, ha, ha, no I didn't," said Japhet disbelievingly.

"Or the ones ..." I started to say, but Japhet had stormed off in a huff, not quite sure if we were pulling his leg or not.

Needless to say, it wasn't long before our old neighbours heard about all the animals gathering around the ark. They left the village to have a look for themselves and then they began openly hunting and killing them for their exotic skins and meat. I had never seen Father as angry as when he first heard about this; he was absolutely furious, but they were too far away and too cunning for him to do much about it. So he stomped off up the hill for a session of prolonged prayer, meditation and divine guidance.

On his return to the ark he said that from now on we had better start guarding the animals as soon as they arrived, especially the more unusual-looking ones and all of us must do our utmost to keep them safe.

"Every species which is new to us and is destroyed by the hunters will be gone for ever. There may be others somewhere in the world but, unless they arrive in time to come onto the ark with us, they will not survive," he warned us, grim-faced. "This is an extremely serious situation and it could put our plans in jeopardy."

"God's plans," muttered Ham with quiet defiance.

With this in mind, Ham was instructed to make plans for their safekeeping. He decided that the best solution would be for someone to make regular checks on the animals throughout the day and night, to see that as far as possible all the new animals were safe. As that would mean checking all over the plains and the woods, we decided to use a pair of hardy desert horses Ham had recently come across. He had already spoken longingly of his desire to ride one of them and now, with the final preparations done, his chance had arrived and he took his pick.

Ham didn't know much about animals, but he thought that the male was likely to be the most difficult, so he chose the mare. He approached her slowly with a handful of tempting herbs, holding a rudimentary bridle that he had made out of leather and reed thongs, out of sight behind his back. For a moment it looked as if the stallion was going to object to this interference with his mare but, after looking Ham over with haughty disdain, he lowered his head and returned to pulling at some of the last tufts of grass.

The only animals Ham had ever ridden before were our docile donkeys and the mule, so the rest of us downed tools and looked on with interest and anticipation. The mare that he had chosen looked a little flighty to me; her ears flickered back and forth and she nervously snatched the herbs from his hand, flashed the whites of her eyes and immediately swung her hindquarters towards him. With a quiet curse he tried again, making a grab for her mane, but quick as a flash she pulled away from him. He tried again and this time she managed to tread on his foot. There is not much protection in thin leather sandals, so this made him hop about in agony, while the rest of us tried not to laugh. Then he tried and failed to loop the reins over her head as she shied away from him again.

After this had gone on for some time, Japhet suggested that the rest of us should try to help by cornering the mare into a space from which she could not escape. When we finally managed to do this, the mare seemed to realise that the game was up and was surprisingly docile when Ham put the bridle over her head. Anael held the reins and stroked the mare's neck to calm her, while Japhet gave Ham a leg up, but when the hem of his robes flapped against the mare's sides it obviously startled her. She immediately swung round in a tight circle with Ham clinging on round her neck and started to buck vigorously. With his weight already forward,

Ham didn't stand a chance and he went flying through the air, landing on the ground with a bone-jolting thump.

At first, no one dared to so much as smile, but when Ham had flown through the air several more times, there was such a guffaw from Father that the rest of us could no longer control ourselves and we all started to laugh. It seemed to have been such a long time since anything particularly funny had happened that all of us, including the three strangers, laughed and laughed until our sides ached and the tears rolled down our cheeks.

Then Salit led one of our old donkeys over to him, which made us all laugh even more and even Ham saw the funny side of it. In the end one of the strangers, Anael, who had helped him to calm the mare in the beginning, managed to quieten her down enough for him to mount up and stay there. Then, perched precariously on the mare's back, Ham set off in fits and starts for the river plain to check on the safety of the new arrivals. At one stage he looked back at us and grinned, optimistically giving us the thumbs up. It would be a miracle if they both returned to the camp together I thought, but somehow they did.

Despite the extra pressure of trying to keep the constant stream of new arrivals safe, we managed a final burst of energy to finish off the ark's interior. Gradually the familiar sounds of sawing and hammering grew less and less, until finally everything that we could possibly think of seemed to have been done. This part of Father's plan was complete and one by one as we finally finished our work, we put down our tools in a pile at the bottom of the gangplank and there was peace at last.

Then something extremely unexpected happened. The three strangers, Kafziel, Samael and Anael, left. They just disappeared, without saying goodbye to any of us, which upset us all. They had been our workmates and companions for so many years by this time that we just assumed they would stay with us as nothing had ever been said about them leaving. Nobody saw them go and none of us had any idea that they were even thinking of leaving.

"Their work was done," said Father, which seemed rather heart-less to the rest of us.

The way he said it made me wonder just for a moment if Father knew more about them than he was letting on? But he said no more, and I knew him well enough to know when a question would be unwise.

Although they had been very welcome helpers and companions, it is worth remembering that we never found out anything about them. Somehow, without being offensive or unfriendly in any way, they remained an absolute mystery. They never said anything about where they came from, where they might be going, or what they had done or what they were going to do and we never asked. We had grown so used to them and genuinely fond of them, that we knew we would miss their presence terribly. Our wives would miss them just as much and felt as sad and hurt by their sudden departure as we did. Even Nahlat had to wipe away a tear.

"How could they just go and leave us like that, without saying anything?" wailed Arisisah. "It is such a cruel thing to do. How could they just go?"

Then, just inside the door of the ark, we saw a small carving that had not been there before. In the wood of the doorpost, one of them had carved a dove with a leaf in its beak; we could only presume it was their goodbye to us.

For a long time after their departure, just catching a glance of the little carving made the tears well up in my eyes. We owed them so much and I missed their company. If we had not been so frantically busy with the final preparations, we would have felt their absence even more keenly, but we were all run off our feet and during the days that followed their departure we just didn't have the time to feel more than fleetingly sad. Without a doubt, their help had halved the time it took us to build the ark, perhaps even more than that, but even so it had taken all of us many, many years of extremely hard work to complete.

Arisisah, who was particularly sad at their leaving, worried about their future. She finally asked Father the question that all of us had tried to avoid thinking about.

"What will happen to them when the flood comes? They helped us for all these years but then didn't remain with us to take advantage of the safety of the ark for themselves."

Father broke the melancholy silence that ensued as we all pondered on their possible fate.

"They will be safe," he said.

And the way he said it was both comforting and authoritative, and at the time we all accepted what he said without asking for further explanation. Later on when we had time on our hands we couldn't help wondering how Father could have been so sure.

The Concept of Time in the Bible

Controversy surrounds the concept of time in the Bible, from the beginning of the Book of Genesis where the creation is described, onwards. This is largely because up until the time of King David, 1,000BC, no historically verifiable events are described. Before this the only measure of time is by generations, the lengths of which were by no means uniform. Some of the characters in the Old Testament are recorded as having lived for hundreds of years, others not.

The earlier events in the Bible were described and handed down by word of mouth and not recorded in writing until hundreds if not thousands of years after they had happened, so it is highly likely that the details of the events may have become distorted in the telling.

There is no known documentation of Hebrew timekeeping at this period, but it would certainly have been influenced by the Egyptians. They used lunar calendars and the annual cycle of the Nile flooding, movements of the sun and shadows it cast, and at night or times of poor visibility, they used hourglasses and water clocks.

While Creationists believe that God created the earth in a matter of days others, including St Augustine, the renowned 4th century theologian, believed that the 'days of creation' is a figurative description, meaning long indeterminate periods of time. In the Koran, time on earth is compared with time in wormholes (one day on earth being the equivalent to 50,000 years).

But, in theory at least, the order in which God is described as having created the earth in the Old Testament book of Genesis is logical and consistent with modern evolutionary scientific thinking.

It is thought that Noah's flood occurred some 5,000 years ago, probably between 2,000 and 3,000BC. This calculation was made by adding up the ages of Shem's descendants from the birth of his son Arphaxad, which is recorded as being two years after the flood, to the birth of Abraham, in approximately 2,000BC. This may be a more reliable method than prior to the flood because, after the flood, God decreed that the normal span of a man's life should be no more than 120 years, whereas before the flood a man's recorded lifespan could vary by hundreds of years.

The longest life recorded in the Bible is that of Methuselah, who we are told lived for 969 years.

In the legends of ancient Mesopotamia, which were transcribed before the Bible, there are tales of people or so-called 'kings' who lived before the flood, some of whom are said to have had a lifespan of thousands of years. It was believed that these kings were originally the messengers of the gods with human attributes. The Mesopotamian gods ruled over every aspect of life and had intricate genealogies; pleasing these gods was extremely important and people looked to the priests to help them do this. When Noah began telling people there was only one God, it was antagonising and frightening for them, as it challenged their core beliefs.

☙❧

Chapter 8

❖

So with the ark finished at last we were left wondering what now? The only rain there had been over the last few months was the occasional short shower, which was quite normal for the time of year. Now, to be honest, I was torn between dreading the horrors of the flood that Father had predicted and a guilty desire to see it actually happen. Just to show all the doubters that he had been right all along.

But supposing it had been a mistake on Father's part, or a test of faith, or just a giant hoax, our family would be in a very awkward situation indeed. We no longer had a home; we had got rid of nearly all our domestic animals, bartered away most of our possessions and fallen out with almost everyone who was left from our old life in the village. Everything we had in the world was on the ark now and we were surrounded by an increasing number of unfamiliar animals, all of which needed feeding and protecting from marauding hunters in the shape of our former neighbours. They no longer cared what we thought of them, they just wanted the exotic skins and meat of the new arrivals. And the fact that we had to do our best to prevent this happening did not increase our popularity very much either.

And all we could do was wait.

But we didn't have to wait for long.

Suddenly, for no particular reason that any of us could fathom, Father decided that it was time to start loading all the animals onto the ark. None of us knew why, but it was never any use questioning Father when he was in one of his dynamic moods, although I could see that Ham was about to start arguing with him about the wisdom of doing this now. He looked at Japhet quizzically and then at the sky with exaggerated interest, but Japhet just shrugged and I knew better than to say anything. So we just got on with it, as we usually did in those days.

"Lots of animals penned up on the ark in this heat, what a great idea," Ham muttered under his breath.

But shortly afterwards, when we saw Father starting to dig up all his precious vine plants from the edge of the clearing, we were finally convinced that something really was going to happen. They were the only precious belongings that he had left and he had tended them carefully ever since we began building the ark. He started by taking down the protective fence he had built around them and then he began to gently unwind all the tendrils of the vines from their stakes before painstakingly replanting them all in large clay containers, which we helped him to carry safely on board.

After that, we had all the animals to cope with. And while we were wondering exactly where to start and how to go about it, I swear even more arrived and seemed to be moving closer and closer to the ark. We no longer questioned why we had built such a large vessel; now we worried that it might not be large enough. Looking at them all milling about, we wondered if we could possibly fit them all into the ark.

"The only possible outcome of all this is pandemonium," said Japhet glumly.

Then there was the added complication that some of the animals were to go on board in sevens, not pairs. We had forgotten all about this, but Father explained that the surplus animals were to be sacrificed to God for his mercy, at "the appropriate time", whenever that might be. This obviously accounted for the seven sheep, goats and other domestic animals that he had insisted on when we were bartering for them with our neighbours.

"Well, if we don't sacrifice them, we can always eat the extra ones," suggested Ham hopefully.

"Do you think when it comes to it we'll have to sacrifice the best of the animals to God, or do we keep the best for breeding?" Japhet mused.

How did he manage to think up such complications at a time like this I wondered?

"Good point, but let's worry about that when the time comes," I said. "Father will know what to do and in the meantime we'd better start trying to get all these animals onto the ark."

As well as the animals, we had to get the birds on board and onto their long perches in the roof. All we had to do was get them there. There seemed to be birds of every shape, size and colour absolutely everywhere – in the trees, pecking on the ground amongst the animals and generally flitting about; some of them were even using the animals as a moving perch. Only the larger ones were less active. The vultures glowered down at us all from the surrounding rocks, their wings furled around them like cloaks, and the eagles soared above the clearing scanning the ground below for prey. To keep them from swooping on the smaller animals destined for the ark, we had been lobbing small stones at them, but now that we wanted them to come onto the ark and I wasn't quite sure how they would react to the change in tactics. We hadn't even considered the really large birds, such as the ostriches, rheas and emus that strutted about confidently amongst the animals and didn't seem to want to perch in trees or on rocks, let alone in the roof of the ark. To start with we had naively assumed that all the birds would fly aboard, but of course it didn't work out quite like that.

We had already worked out that it would be best if the largest of the animals were to go in the bottom of the ark and the small and medium ones on the middle deck. That meant there was no real alternative but for us to have our living quarters there as well, a prospect that Nahlat and Mother had never been particularly enthusiastic about.

"The noise and the smell, do they really have to be so close to us and what about the dangerous ones?"

"Well believe me, if any of us could have thought of a better alternative we would have used it," I replied rather sharply.

We left the birds for the time being and started with the animals, there seemed to be hundreds of them. As they pressed on towards the ark some of them started to jostle each other and we obviously needed to try to create some sort of order. By now most of the larger ones were aimlessly wandering around in the clearing, which their hooves and feet had reduced to a dust bowl. The vegetation had virtually gone and it was almost completely covered with animal droppings. Fortunately, the heat of the sun quickly dried everything up, or the smell would have been unbearable. Every now and then one of the animals would stop to tug at one of the few remaining tufts of vegetation and cause a pile-up behind them and even the smallest altercation caused much squealing and pushing. All we could do was pray that this wouldn't escalate and cause a major upset, which would have resulted in carnage amongst the smaller animals.

Father had stationed himself on the hill above us and was blowing a horn to summon the animals to the ark. To our consternation even more began to appear over the horizon and make their way towards us.

"Can't someone stop him? Surely we've got more than enough already?" asked Japhet desperately. "We really don't need him to encourage even more of them."

But by now everyone was so busy that we just had to leave him to it.

"If more of them come they are obviously meant to go onto the ark, so I expect he knows what he's doing," said Arisisah.

"I should damn well hope so," said Ham.

So now not only did we have to get this heaving mass of animals onto the ark, there was another problem as well. Some of the animals, but fortunately not all that many, looked virtually identical to each other and there were others where the male and the female were so unalike that they could have been from different species. We had to decide if this meant that they actually were different, or just a slight variation of the same breed, or even a pair at all. Japhet volunteered to make the decisions. "I haven't sat for years gazing at sheep and not learned how to tell every one of them apart, let alone distinguish the difference between breeds, however similar they might look. If they're the same I'll just choose the fittest pair, simple."

"Well don't ask me," said Ham. "I'm not going to argue with you, I've got no idea. All sheep look exactly the same to me."

At this, Japhet raised his eyebrows with mock horror.

"Me too," I said. "I've had very little to do with animals, as you know."

Japhet's confidence was heartening, so the rest of us were only too happy to stand aside and delegate this task to him.

Almost immediately a problem arose, when we saw the quaggas, okapis and zebras waiting at the bottom of the gangplank. With their striking stripy markings they were easy to pick out from the throng. Ham had mustered them to the front of the general herd and now all six of them were milling around, waiting for me to send them on board.

"Stop right there," shouted Japhet. "What's all this? And are you all the same or slightly different?"

"Er, I don't think they talk you know," Ham shouted up at him.

Unfortunately all this shouting startled them and one of the zebras stopped in its tracks, stamped its feet impatiently and snorted, before backing into the two quaggas following behind. They all looked very similar to me, except that the quaggas' stripes seemed to have run out a bit towards their hindquarters and the rest of their coat was rather more yellow than white. A fight was in the offing and, as we later learned to our cost, zebras have very bad tempers and quaggas not much better. In a less fraught situation, without all the other animals milling around, it would have been easier to see that the okapis actually looked very different from the others, with their sloping shoulders, smaller heads, relatively large ears and timid ways.

Then suddenly, as if to settle the matter, the zebras and the quaggas rushed on board and, as they pushed past, I saw that the male zebra had his ears back and was showing his displeasure by nipping his unfortunate mate in the shoulder. She in turn squealed with pain and surprise and in trying to avoid him, she slipped and almost fell from the top of the gangplank. I couldn't help hoping that I wouldn't be in charge of them on board as they looked like trouble to me. Meanwhile all this commotion had alarmed the two okapis so much that they turned around and melted back into the bustling throng of animals. We didn't see them again until the following day, when everything had calmed down and they were amongst the last animals to go on board.

Once we got going, a rough system evolved quite quickly. Ham stayed on the ground, a scarf tied over his nose and mouth as protection from all the dust being kicked up, doing his best to drive the animals towards the bottom of the gangplank where I stood trying to organise them into going on board in some kind of order. I had hoped that our two sheepdogs might have been useful here, but they were completely overwhelmed by the chaos and the size of some of the animals and had slunk away to hide under the ark.

Japhet stood at the top of the gangplank as a safeguard to replication. It was also up to him to shout out which level they should go on, so that Nahlat and Salit could encourage them into their designated living quarters. Needless to say, things went far from smoothly and there was either a huge rush of animals all at once, or a large gap whilst Ham and I tried to get some recalcitrant beast to venture up the gangplank, instead of trying to swerve back into the mass of waiting animals and hold everything up. I didn't dare imagine what might be happening inside where I heard the frequent clatter of hooves on the wooden floors and Nahlat and Salit shouting rather desperately.

Ham thought Japhet and I should change places. "Surely it would be better to decide things before the animals actually get as far as the gangplank?"

But Japhet disagreed, saying he needed the animals to be out of the crowd at the bottom of the gangplank in order to have a proper look at them. Ham just shrugged and then Father began to shout at us wondering what the hold up was, so we just carried on.

Occasionally Father came down to sort out disputes amongst the throng of waiting animals that still tailed back out of sight. It was important that none of the animals got too anxious or upset, which might have started a mass stampede away from the ark. The smallest incident could quickly have escalated into a widespread panic and of course it would have been a disaster if any of the animals got hurt.

Added to this, Father was particularly anxious that Mother should not to see all of the creatures that were going on board, because he knew that if she saw some of her future travelling companions she would probably refuse to go onto the ark herself. Over the last few years, poor Mother's patience and good nature had been sorely tried by the dramatic change in our circumstances. So in order to distract her, Father had asked Arisisah to help her check through some of the supplies for one last time. This kept them both out of the way and diverted Mother's attention away from her prospective shipmates, which was the real object of the exercise, as everything on the ark had already been checked again and again.

With some of the animals, like the tortoises, it was impossible to tell male and female apart, so Japhet simply lifted a few of them on as spares. "Better safe than sorry," he said as he carefully handed them over one by one to Salit. With these indistinguishable species, letting a few extra on board just in case seemed to be the best solution, especially if they were on the small side.

"We can always sacrifice some of them," he said.

"Or eat them," said Ham. "But mind you don't let too many extra on, or there won't be enough room for them all and, if that happens, they'll probably start eating each other."

By far the most distressing situations arose on the rare occasions when we did have to turn animals away. A male might arrive with his harem of females and a quick decision had to be made; Japhet would look them over, send the male on board first and then choose the healthiest-looking female and send her on board behind him. This could be an upsetting process, with the rejected animals crying out pitifully and making desperate attempts to barge on board and join their mate.

"Thank heavens there are only two elephants," Japhet said. "There is a limit to the success of this whole selection process and I think that might be it."

"Actually, there are four of them," said Ham. "Father's horn has attracted another two, but they have smaller ears."

"Are you joking?" exclaimed Japhet.

But he wasn't; there were four elephants. Two of them did have smaller ears and they seemed to be a bit smaller and less intimidating altogether.

The whole embarkation process was chaotic, but we could only do our best in such difficult circumstances. One thing we did know was that in many species the male was the more handsome-looking and the female the duller, so as long as one of each was chosen, it would all come to the same in the end, or at least we hoped it would. We were under a lot of pressure to get things right but, as Japhet said, if we got it wrong sometimes it couldn't be helped. "And frankly who would know anyway?"

"God of course," said Ham quick as a flash.

Typically, Ham was right in the thick of it near the base of the gangplank, pushing and shoving where necessary, cajoling the more nervous animal to manoeuvre them safely towards me in some kind of order. Some of the animals seemed to be more concerned with food than anything else and were still optimistically searching for their last mouthfuls of vegetation right up to the bottom of the gangplank. To encourage them to move on Ham had no alternative but to whack them on the rump. This startled some of the more highly strung animals who then lurched forwards in alarm, frightening some of the other animals so much that they began to separate from their mates. At this Father roared down from his vantage point on the hillside, "Just go easy there will you, Ham?"

We had never seen, or even heard of, anything like the ostriches, emus and rheas, with their large bodies, long legs and small heads.

When these large birds arrived at the top of the gangplank, even Japhet was totally nonplussed. "Hey, shouldn't you have flown onboard and up to the roof perches like all the others?" he asked. The large birds looked stonily back at him, their heads weaving about on their long necks and their beady eyes blinking at him.

"You can sleep under them if they do ..." muttered Nahlat under her breath.

And indeed, when we looked at them more closely, it was obvious that even if they had any wings, they were far too small to propel their ample bodies very far up into the air.

"Middle deck, then," Japhet shouted at Salit and Nahlat as the stately birds strutted past him into the ark.

"I think you mean lower deck," Nahlat shouted back. "They are far too large for anywhere else ... and too tall," she added, as she looked them up and down.

"Oh all right then, sorry," Japhet shouted back irritably as he was getting exhausted by then "You decide."

So Nahlat shooed them down to the lower deck where they joined the larger animals; there just didn't seem to be any other solution.

By sundown that day, we were relieved to see that the number of animals on board finally exceeded the ones still left outside and we felt we were getting somewhere. By now, Father had come down the hill and was walking slowly amongst the remaining animals, playing soothing tunes on his flute to keep them calm.

We were all absolutely exhausted and any thought of continuing by candlelight was discounted as the flickering lights would probably have alarmed the animals and anyway we were far too tired to continue.

"A really early start tomorrow is it, then?" asked Father.

"Yes Father," we all replied in unison. By then we were ready to agree to anything in order to stop for the day.

That evening we stayed outside to have our meal. But unfortunately, it wasn't a terribly pleasant experience. The dust created by hundreds of animals' hooves had barely settled which meant that the smallest movement was enough to raise it, making us cough and splutter and ruining our food. Still, we all made the best of it, something we were good at by now. And we even kept quiet when Mother pointed out some small night-flying birds swooping around above us.

"Do you really think she didn't know they were bats?" asked Arisisah.

"No, and nor did I," said Nahlat who had overheard her and started nervously wrapping her robes more tightly around herself. "If I had, I certainly wouldn't have continued to sit there and admire them."

That night Ham volunteered to guard the animals that remained outside in case any of our old neighbours appeared at the last minute with hunting on their minds.

Building the Ark

According to the Old Testament, it took Noah and his sons approximately 120 years to build the ark. It was an extraordinarily large vessel for its time, but of a design that the inexperienced Noah and his sons were able to follow.

God gave Noah the dimensions of the ark and specified that it was to be built from 'Gopherwood', which has never been precisely identified. It may have been a method of processing wood or a type of tree that is extinct. But at the time there must have been plentiful supplies of it available, in order to build a vessel 300 cubits long, 50 cubits wide and 30 cubits high.

A cubit was the standard form of measurement at the time, being the length of a man's forearm from elbow to fingertip (roughly 20 inches). This means that the ark would have been around 137 metres long (450 feet), 23 metres wide (75 feet) and 14 metres (45 feet) high. It was to have three decks and the whole vessel was to be coated with pitch, inside and out, to waterproof and preserve it.

Elsewhere in the Bible we are told that metal tools of iron and bronze had been in use for hundreds of years by the time the ark was built, originally developed by Tubal Cain, a descendant of Adam's son Cain who slew his brother Abel. So it would have been possible to drill holes in wood, saw planks and use either wooden pegs or metal nails to secure the structure of the ark.

ॐॐॐ

Chapter 9

⊰◈⊱

As soon as the sun rose the next day Father had us all up and working again. We thought we'd start by trying to get some of the smaller water-loving animals on board. This meant Ham, Japhet and I scrambling about in the nearby stream, getting soaked to the skin, trying to scoop up elusive and slippery creatures of every description into leather bags and slings to transport them safely back to the ark. Most of them were extremely tricky to deal with, easily evading our clumsy efforts to grab them by gliding away from us under water. They clearly felt vulnerable at the prospect of leaving their watery habitat and weren't going to give in that easily.

"These frogs," shouted Japhet, holding out his arms out stiffly in front of him as yet another slithered between his fingers and plopped back into the stream, "they're impossibly slippery. I'm never going to be able to keep hold of them and I think they're actually enjoying giving me the slip." But he did finally succeed in grabbing a handful of them from the water and took them onto the ark; their thin legs and long feet dangling limply through his fingers, feebly kicking the air and struggling ineffectually, in one last effort to escape.

The otters and turtles were next; the turtles had a nasty bite and when one of them determinedly attached itself to Ham's thumb, the pain made him curse as fiercely as he ever had. The otters just wanted to play, their sleek brown bodies gliding away from us and then curling around our legs before vanishing into the deeper parts of the stream. But we caught them in the end and made our way back to the ark, all three of us soaked to the skin. Then just as we were leaving we saw two brown furry heads protruding from the water. "Oh no, not more otters," groaned Japhet, "and they're big ones too, just look at those teeth." In spite of this Ham bravely made a lunge towards them, but they easily evaded him.

"Oh never mind," Japhet said, "We've got our quota now, so let's just leave them to it."

Later on however, we saw two large brown animals waddle up the bank and out of the river towards the ark, dripping with water. Once they were out of the water we could see that they had unusually prominent front teeth and large, flat tails. They were beavers and fortunately it seemed they had decided to give in and make their own way on board.

The seals were also keeping themselves cool in the stream and were quite unlike anything we had ever seen before; their bodies gleamed like metal as the sun caught them. Looking at the size of them, I prayed that we wouldn't have to go into the stream again and attempt to catch them. As Ham stood on the bank looking at the huge male seal with his bulging eyes and whiskers, he shouted: "Remind you of anyone, Japhet?"

"Nahlat's Father?" replied Japhet at once, quickly looking around to check that she was out of earshot. And with that, he picked up a large stick with which he drove them out of the stream and onto the ark. "Child's play when you know how," he said grinning. "Actually, it's all in the angle that you approach them at: get it right and you can get them to do anything; get it wrong and you just drive them away from you. Works with almost anything actually, horses, cows, dogs . . . You aim for a point just behind their shoulder, to drive them forward, then a point slightly in front of that and they will usually let you go up to them."

We had left most of the birds alone to fly around the clearing outside the ark although, to be honest, we didn't have much option and so far only a few of them had chosen to come on board by themselves and perch in the roof. Now with most of the animals settled on board, the noise had died down and we could hear all those that remained outside twittering and screeching in the branches of the trees around the clearing, darting about far out of our reach. It wasn't really surprising that they preferred to congregate on the leafy boughs of the remaining trees rather than the stark-looking perches on board the ark. We realised that we were going to have to make the roof area look more appealing if we were ever going to entice them all on board.

"Why don't we cut down some foliage and tie it to the perches, so that it looks more homely for them?" I suggested.

"More work," Ham groaned.

But Japhet and Father agreed with me, it had to be done, so we fetched our saws and set to work. It didn't make things any easier that the lowest branches of the surrounding trees were quite bare of leaves by now, stripped of all their foliage by hungry animals. We had to climb up to a height where the leaves were out of reach from the ground before we could cut down any of the leafy branches that we needed. Then we dragged them back to the ark and pulled them up to the roof perches with ropes and secured them in place. Our efforts made the birds' living quarters look much more homely and hopefully more attractive to the birds that remained out of our reach in the clearing. As we pulled the branches past them, the giraffes took the opportunity to have a good nibble at some of the leaves, but once we had hauled them high up into the roof they were safely out of reach.

"I can see those two are going to be a pest," said Japhet. "They seem to be able to reach almost anywhere and they're already pulling the bedding out of some of the other animals' stalls."

"I saw them have a good look at Father's vines as they went by," said Ham.

"That had better be all they do, or there really will be trouble," I said.

"But they have such beautiful eyes," said Arisisah, "I think I could forgive them almost anything."

"Then let's hope Father agrees with you," said Ham.

Somehow, during all these last-minute preparations, Father had managed to keep Mother out of the way. She appeared to be doing a lot of resting at the moment I thought, although how on earth this was possible with all the clattering up and down the gang-plank and the shouting, I really didn't know. Maybe she had seen the crocodiles or the pigs coming on board and fainted.

The necessity to cut foliage for the birds' perches was the saving of two very strange animals. We found them both hanging upside down from two strong branches in a shady part of the wood and they appeared to be fast asleep. One of them was actually snoring quietly.

"Quite extraordinary," said Father going a little closer and inspecting them cautiously. "Does anyone know what they are?"

"I believe they are sloths, Father," said Japhet.

"Well they'd better get a move on," said Father "or they'll be left behind. Wake them up please, Japhet."

Gingerly, Japhet put out his hand and touched one of the sloths, but nothing happened. He gently tugged a bit of its long fur, which was of course dangling downwards ... still nothing. Then Ham gently prodded one of them with a stick, which finally produced a huge sigh and then a gentle moan. He prodded it a bit harder at which there was a juddering snore and a huge yawn releasing a gale of foul breath, before the sloth went back to sleep.

"Oh, how disgusting," cried Ham, jumping back. "What are we going to do with them?"

In the end, when we had failed to wake up either of the sloths, it seemed that there was nothing for it but to leave them behind. Then Japhet had an idea – we could simply cut off the branches they were hanging from and carry them onto the ark. The dead weight of the two sleeping animals made them surprisingly heavy but we managed it.

Once we had lugged them on board to almost the last available stall, we wedged the branches into the joists, with them still resolutely hanging from them, upside down. The final irony was that this did actually wake one of them up. And then he – or was it she? – let go slowly from the branch with one paw and then another and it was then that we noticed it had fearsome claws. It eased itself to the bottom of its stall and did a surprisingly large deposit then, slightly faster than it had descended; it hauled itself back onto its branch and fell asleep again. There followed an unseemly argument among us, as to which of us should clear up after it.

"Don't use the dung chute yet," ordered Japhet. "Take it off the ark and well away from here, or the smell will be horrible."

In the light of what was to come, this was a ridiculous suggestion and quite unnecessary.

Whilst most of the birds and animals were easy to spot, there were other creatures that were almost too small to see. The insects and the "creepy crawlies" as Nahlat called them included moths, spiders, ants, woodlice and flies that varied in size from quite large to virtually invisible.

"Do we really have to save the flies?" Japhet complained. "I don't think there is anything on earth more annoying than flies and we'll never have a better chance to get rid of them. Just let me squash these two and those ones over there. If we take them on board there won't be just a few for long."

But Father said, "No, we can't afford to lose anything, not even the flies. They are all part of God's plan."

So Japhet shrugged and the flies survived.

Personally, if I had been given the chance, I would have left all the snakes and the rats and mice behind, but in the end none of them caused us much trouble. The rats and mice did eat quite large amounts of our grain stores, but what could we expect? It wasn't any worse than things would have been on land. And, as for the snakes, to everyone's enormous relief they nearly all coiled up neatly and went to sleep almost as soon as they had slithered into their compartments.

"Make sure they are shut in tight," said Nahlat with a shudder.

"And there's no need to mention them to your Mother," said Father. "Let's just hope she doesn't see them until it's too late."

Of course there were lots of hitches. The pandas for instance had a roomy stall, but only one of them would go into it. The other dug its claws into the passage floor and then the doorposts of the stall and in spite of all our efforts pushing and pulling, it simply refused to follow its mate inside.

"What do you think is the matter?" Father asked Japhet. "Is it too small for them both, do you think? That one's in there eating quite happily, but this one won't budge."

"Maybe they just don't like each other," suggested Ham. "I suppose there's no reason why they should."

"Well, if that's the case, it's very inconvenient and we are looking at the last two pandas on earth," said Japhet irritably, his tiredness taking its toll. "Ungrateful beasts."

"I think there is an empty stall down at the end of the passage," said Ham. "Let's put her in there for now and try and sort it out later."

But we never did. They obdurately refused to go into the same stall together and spent the entire voyage living apart quite contentedly. They both ate extremely heartily and consequently required a lot of clearing out.

"Oh why won't some animals hibernate when you'd like them to?" Ham moaned later.

Of course it was inevitable that we should have numerous problems with the animals' living quarters and we soon found out that the original arrangements we had made just did not suit them all. Some of the animals arrived together in a group, having travelled from their homelands together and they were unhappy at being split up by size once they were on the ark. But what else could we do? How, for instance, could we house polar bears, who were large and needed to go on the bottom deck, with the white foxes who travelled with them and were middle-deck size? Then there were the penguins, yet more flightless birds that would have preferred to be near the bears and the foxes. It was this sort of thing that we hadn't foreseen that threw our plans out.

Then there were the animals that we had put in suitable enclosures but were so terrified of their new neighbours that they had to be moved. The lions and tigers in particular seemed to intimidate most of the other animals, which was awkward but understandable. In the end, we moved the hippopotamuses and the rhinos in next to them as they were far too large and thick skinned to be nervous of anything, and then everything settled down. The zebras continued to be bad-tempered, only too ready to kick out at each other or anyone else who annoyed them. To keep them calm, Japhet put the elephants next to them and, whenever they misbehaved, one of the elephants would lean over and gently put a restraining trunk between them.

From the very beginning we knew how important it was to try and make everyone as comfortable as possible, so however inconvenient it was we sometimes had to swap them around. It was never easy, as it was nearly always something small afraid of something large, so a straight swap was often out of the question. It meant that we had to change numerous other stalls as well, in order to keep all the animals happy. We found out the hard way that it was far more difficult to get an animal out of a stall when it had settled in, than to get it to go in in the first place, unless of course it was a panda. As a last resort, if an animal really got upset, Arisisah put some appropriate herbs in its feed to calm it down and make it more amenable.

One of the most unusual groups of creatures to arrive together came from the East, such a great distance from the ark that none of us had ever seen or heard of anything like them. They really were beyond our wildest imaginings. The kangaroos and wallabies had extraordinarily large back legs and, as if this wasn't strange enough, they had bulky pouches on their stomachs from which they unpacked some extremely strange travelling companions. The oddest of these were the platypuses, who were definite contenders for the strangest creatures on the ark and, I can tell you, they had some competition. These platypuses had small furry bodies, a large flat tail and a beak like a duck and were very fond of water, so much so that we were always fishing them out of the larger animals' drinking troughs, where we often found them swimming round and round or scrabbling at the sides, trapped and unable to get out.

We had other unexpected problems as well. There was the single phoenix, disappointingly only one of them had turned up. Without a doubt it was the most beautiful of all the birds on the ark, with its red breast and long tail of iridescent feathers. However there was one big drawback: it was absolutely obsessed by fire. It was always playing around with the embers of our one and only fireplace and it became such a pest that there were times when we thought either it or the fire would have to go.

As Japhet said irritably, "I didn't go through all this to be burnt to death by the antics of that damned bird."

Finally it disappeared and we presumed that it really had burnt itself to death and I'm afraid that we couldn't help thinking that, sad as it was; at least the problem had sorted itself out. But mysteriously not long afterwards it was back again and still fooling around with embers of our fire. If anyone tried to catch it, it simply flew up to the perches like a spark, far out of our reach. So after that we had to hope for the best, just as we had had to do with so many other things.

Then there were the armadillos, with their strange, scaly skins that rolled themselves up into a ball like huge woodlice shutting their shells with a sharp snap when they were alarmed. We had wrongly classified them as middle-deck animals when in fact they needed to be in the bottom of the ark, not because of their size, but because the slightly damper atmosphere down there suited them better. Every now and then during the day, one of us had to wedge them into a corner of their pen with some branches to give them a rest, otherwise they rolled around endlessly, curled up in a ball, irritating the other animals with the thump, thump noise they made, bumping into the sides of their stall.

The very last animals of all to arrive were the yetis and the yaks. The yaks had long icy white hair hanging nearly to the ground and fearsome curved horns; the yetis were … well, rather like us, really, although they didn't wear clothes and were taller, broader and much hairier, conversing in grunts not words: rather like Ham when he was in a sulk, as Japhet wryly observed. When they arrived, their appearance gave us quite a turn and their first sight of us obviously shocked them too. They both stood at the top of the gangplank, heads down, shoulders hunched, cautiously peering into the ark and then, giving a small grunt, they suddenly shot inside and disappeared.

"How very strange," said Father. "Do you think they will be all right?"

"Do you think they should be here at all?" asked Ham. "They do look a bit like that odd family that used to live down near the river." Even through his exhaustion, Father couldn't help but smile broadly and nod in agreement. We waited for a while longer to see if there would be any more latecomers, but nothing else arrived.

One of the last things we had to do was to drive off all the other animals that had been hanging around the ark with no prospect of coming with us. Their constant calls of distress from outside were upsetting the animals on board and we couldn't think of anything else to do.

"Straight into the arms of our lovely neighbours," said Japhet glumly.

"Yum, yum," said Ham rather heartlessly.

It seemed unutterably sad to think of those poor animals. Was that really all we could do for them? Father must have seen my expression. "We have done our best Shem, that's all we can do. We have all had a great deal to put up with these last years."

"But at least we're not going to be killed and eaten by our neighbours," I couldn't help blurting out.

He was right of course, it had been hard and at times things had been extremely difficult for all of us. Even Salit, normally such a placid and cheerful person, was driven to lament that she had not married me to live a life like this. It was only with great restraint that I avoided the argument that would have ensued if I had pointed out that the alternative might not have been terribly attractive either.

Working together for so long had changed all of us and altered some of the family dynamics and alliances. Mother and Arisisah

94

had formed a particularly close bond, both of them helping and encouraging the other. But they were very different: Mother was a dutiful wife and accepted her place was at Father's side, although sometimes nowadays her support was more like quiet resignation; Arisisah was more of a dreamer and as long as she was near Japhet she was content. With Mother's help and experience, she matured into a calm and supportive wife for Japhet, who was inclined to worry about everything now that he had more responsibility than a few sheep.

After his quiet life as a shepherd with plenty of time for solitary contemplation, he had been forced to integrate with the rest of us and become a full-time member of the family group building the ark, which had been especially hard for him. He had never been a very sociable man and, until all this happened, he had been quite content to spend time on his own with just his dog for company and Arisisah to welcome him when he returned from the plains. But as Father had predicted right at the start, he became a fine organiser, with a real talent for thinking of solutions to the problems that occurred daily.

Ham was very different: proud, stubborn and outspoken, he frequently tested Father's patience to the absolute limit, as he had done all his life. But once he knuckled down to the huge task we had been set, nobody was a harder worker and his ability to see the funny side of almost anything cheered us up when we were feeling dispirited and tired.

Nahlat had found it the hardest of all to accept this extraordinary change from the married life that she had been expecting with Ham. It wasn't that she complained, she just seemed to disappear when things got too much for her. Although it was never that hard to tell where she was as we could always hear the noise of her violent sneezing, brought on by the hay and the animals. Ham found it was wisest to leave her be when she withdrew like that and Mother had learned long ago not to try and take her to task about anything, unless it was absolutely necessary.

Looking back now, I suppose Father had the hardest time of all, although none of us really appreciated it at the time. We were all so busy coping with our own problems. He not only had the responsibility of getting the ark built, which was exhausting for all of us, he also had to contend with the constant ridicule of his neighbours and the scepticism of his own family. His faith in God had driven him to do the unthinkable, to the extent that he even ignored the opinions of the person who had always been his closest confidante, his wife, who was as doubtful about the ark as everyone else. He tried hard to be cheerful and encouraging but he was a serious man at heart and at times his eyes had a look of unutterable sadness. Maybe he was contemplating his failure to convince his neighbours and fellow villagers to take him seriously.

The death of his Father, Lamech, only a few years before the completion of the ark had been a great loss for him. Because of his ingenuity and good humour, all of us loved and respected our grandfather and he had always been a great support to Father, even when he first heard about the ark. Although he later confided to me that even he had had serious concerns about Father's sanity at the time. Of all Lamech's grandsons, Ham was the most like him, which was probably why Father was so tolerant with him.

But Father did have God to talk to, which he did several times a day and that was his greatest strength. Don't get me wrong; by now Father's unshakeable conviction and the extraordinary things that had happened had convinced all of us to believe in his one God, how could we not? But not to the same extent as Father, who was always absolutely steadfast in his belief. The rest of us just didn't have his unwavering faith in what we were doing. I was not used to being made fun of, none of us were, and we all absolutely hated it when our neighbours mocked us for building the ark.

Finally we had carried out every last-minute task that we could think of and all the animals were on board the ark, fed and watered. Only then did we have time to sit down and relax and of course we immediately started to remember some of the things we had left behind or thought we might need and it seemed quite reasonable to us that we should want to go back to the village to fetch them. But on hearing this, Father flew into one of his worst rages and told us that we were not to return to the village on any account, no matter what we had forgotten or how important it might seem to us. He gave us strict instructions that none of us were to venture far away from the ark again and that was the will of God.

"Why?" asked Ham, but Father had already turned on his heel and disappeared.

So that was that.

By now all of us were so used to working hard that now that we had the chance to ease up a bit we actually found it difficult to stop and relax, even Japhet. But Father told us to make the most of this opportunity to rest while we still had the chance. The only thing he did allow us to do was to let out some of the grass-eating animals, a few at a time, to have a final feast of growing vegetation along the banks of the stream.

"This is as exciting as watching pitch dry," said Ham as he wandered along the stream accompanied by two goats on thin bits of twine that constantly became entangled in bushes while they made the most of this last chance to eat some of the rather unappetising clumps of vegetation that remained.

Fortunately by now, although the roof was still open, nearly all the birds had congregated quite happily on the vast perches in the roof of the ark. And apart from a little flitting about and rearrangement, they no longer seemed inclined to venture very far away. The only exception to this were the two magpies, who refused to enter the ark at all and sat on top of the roof screaming their harsh cries down at the rest of us below.

"I just don't know what it is about everything that is black and white on this ark," said Ham, who was obviously thinking about the zebras and the pandas, "but they all seem to be blooming awkward."

But finally after fretting at our unaccustomed inactivity for a day or two, we began to relax and appreciate the chance to reflect, knowing that everything that needed doing had been done. Everything had been prepared, everything was ready, but still nothing was happening and not a single drop of rain had fallen. After all this, surely Father couldn't be wrong?

But no, it seemed that he was right.

Why?

In the first chapters of the Old Testament it says, "The wickedness of humankind was great on the earth, and every inclination of the thoughts of their hearts was on evil continually."

But it should be emphasised that one almost insurmountable problem was the people's belief in numerous gods. Man is unique in his need to worship and people found it hugely difficult to comprehend that all the actions and stories they had always believed came from many gods, could have come from just one God. They found Noah's idea of monotheism (one God) beyond belief.

Their gods had specific spheres of power, needs such as food sleep and clothing, and were often found to be unreliable and incompetent; all very human attributes. Ideas such as repentance and forgiveness were alien to those who believed in many gods – polytheism.

So finally, after giving man a number of chances to redeem himself, God decided to start again. He flooded the earth to annihilate "both man and beast and creeping things and birds of the heavens ... to destroy all flesh, wherein is the breath of life, from under heaven".

Only Noah, a man the Bible says was "righteous in his generation", and his family were to be spared this terrible destruction. The animals were to suffer the same fate, all except for the "seven pairs of every clean animal, and one pair of every kind of unclean animal".

ॐ

Chapter 10

Exactly seven days after we entered the ark, the rain began. It didn't start with a dramatic storm, there was no thunder, nor flash of lightning, it just began to rain. And then it rained, and rained, and rained, on and on. It simply poured down. None of us had ever seen anything like it before. And all the while the wind howled round the ark so fiercely that it was almost impossible to pull the roof shut to keep the inside dry.

The sudden start of the deluge and the ferocity of the wind that blew up took all of us by surprise. This was ironic when you think about it, as we had all been waiting so long, years and years in fact, for the rain to begin. Ham, Japhet and I decided we must brave the storm to have one last look around the clearing and check that we hadn't left anything important behind. The three of us stood hesitantly in the doorway, our robes flapping so hard that it felt as if they might be dragged from our backs, before finally bracing ourselves and dashing down the gangplank into the clearing. The torrential rain immediately plastered our hair to our heads, stuck our robes to our bodies and almost blinded us. The strength of the wind blew branches and unused planks around the clearing as if they were leaves from a tree. It was far too dangerous for us to stay outside for long and, not surprisingly, in those conditions, we couldn't find anything at all that we needed to bring back on board. Our wives stood looking on anxiously from the door of the ark, robes flying out in the wind as they watched us rushing about like headless chickens, dodging the flying debris and buffeted about by the force of the wind and rain.

Once we were safely back on board, we ran around the outside corridors closing all the shutters as quickly as we could to stop the rain driving in and soaking everything. Then we remembered that we still had to raise the gangplank, which was quite a task. It had been built strong enough to support the weight of the largest animals as they boarded, so it was monumentally heavy. Nothing we tried would raise it from the ground; it was so deeply embedded in the earth, which had been churned up by the feet of all the animals. Once it started to rain the thick mud held it down like glue. We finally managed to lift it with the help of the elephants and the oxen all hauling together on support ropes from inside the ark. It was chaos, with much slipping and sliding and contradictory instructions being shouted from all sides. Unfortunately, one of the oxen became so alarmed at all the noise that it started to panic, weaving its head from side to side with its huge horns and finally treading heavily on Japhet's foot, which brought tears to his eyes and curses to his lips that Ham would have been proud of.

While Japhet hopped around in agony, the rest of us had managed to calm the ox down so that we could finish the job. Then finally, using almost superhuman strength, we were able to wind the ropes tightly round and round the two huge wooden keepers on the inside of the ark and the gangplank was securely closed. For the finishing touch, Father insisted that we slap a heavy coat of pitch round the frame of the gangplank to ensure that the ark was absolutely watertight; Ham and Japhet rather reluctantly agreed to do the job together.

Then to Mother's consternation, Father insisted that he should have one last inspection of the ark from the outside. Now the gangplank was sealed shut, he had to lower himself laboriously down to the ground by rope, buffeted by the wind like a feather on a cord and blinded by the rain while Mother watched on anxiously. Unfortunately the downpour almost obscured the ark, even from close to, so like us he soon had to give up. Getting back on board again was an undignified process of half climbing and half being hauled up the side of the ark by Japhet and me. He finally tumbled awkwardly back over the side onto the deck, puce-faced with exertion and covered from head to toe with mud.

"I'm too old for all this," he muttered to himself.

I was downwind and heard him; it sounded uncharacteristically pathetic, as Father had always seemed so strong. I prayed that if Ham saw him he would not make some facetious remark and infuriate Father, but luckily he was still below putting the finishing touches to the pitch round the doorposts of the gangplank. By now the rain was falling so hard that all Father had to do to clean off was to stand on deck with his arms in the air for a few moments until the rain washed him clean. When Mother pointed out some places on his legs that were still muddy he told her to stop fussing and pulled away from her like a naughty child and insisted on going straight inside.

And a bit later, when we looked out through chinks in the shutters, our surroundings had been totally transformed. Water dashed and cascaded down the hillside all around us, raising spray like smoke over the rocks and trees that were still standing, and turning the slopes into a huge, torrential waterfall. The scree on the hillside was being flushed away like sand, momentarily revealing flashes of the gleaming rocks that lay beneath, before being submerged again under the deluge of water and stones that poured down from above. Broken trees that had been ripped up by their roots or snapped like twigs with the force of the water crashed down the slopes until there were hardly any left standing on the whole hillside. A few remained, clinging tenaciously to the rock face, until finally the force of the descending water flung them down the slopes as well. It was quite terrifying to behold.

The violence of this scene shook us all, but the ark stood firm in the centre of the clearing like a huge wooden island and, realising we were safe for now at least, we pulled ourselves together in order to keep all the animals calm. The constant noise of falling rocks, pebbles and trees was unsettling as they continually bombarded the side of the ark, propelled by the force of the water that rampaged down the hillside all around us. Arisisah was run off her feet feeding calming herbs to as many of the terrified

102

animals as she could manage in order to stop them panicking and hurting themselves.

With the noise of the rain hammering on the roof and outer decks, together with the cracks of thunder and flashes of lightning all around the ark, it was almost impossible to think, but we did our best. The inside of the ark resounded to the shrieks, groans and muffled roars of animals panicking in their stalls and it felt like a living nightmare. The birds added to the pandemonium, voicing their anxiety in a hundred different cries, which only added to the general uproar. They were as alarmed as we were by this drastic change of circumstance and every time anything particularly noisy or unexpected happened they panicked again, as did we, I might add.

With such turbulent conditions inside and out to cope with, we didn't have much opportunity to think about those who had mocked Father's warnings and been left behind. But in the rare quieter moments it was hard not to imagine what must have been happening. How could we possibly ignore the terrible fate that must have befallen them all?

I imagined that at first the people in our village would probably have been glad of the rain for their crops as it had been dry for months, and we knew that the fishermen would have rejoiced that the rain was finally swelling the rivers again. But as the rain continued and the water levels rose, there would have come a point when they must surely have remembered Father's warnings and started to worry that his predictions might really be coming true.

Sooner or later they would realise what their fate might be and I, for one, felt ashamed to think that there had been times when I had actually wished for the flood to start, just to show the villagers that Father was right and that he was not the fool that they had thought he was for so long.

The rain was falling so relentlessly that before long the rivers would burst their banks and meet the rivulets and torrents of water running down from the hills towards the village. Then, even if they had wanted to, the villagers would have had no chance of forging their way through the river and the deluge of water up to where the ark was. Very soon the river would be in full flood and impassable, as it had been on a few occasions in the past and,. even if some of them managed to cross the river and then the plains to the hills, the force of the descending water would have made the slopes impossibly slippery and treacherous to climb. We realised with growing dismay that all the people below us would be trapped, with no means of escape. Like our neighbours, we had always thought ourselves lucky to be able to collect our water from a nearby river. Now, instead of providing everyone with a good living, it would be instrumental in drowning them all.

The huge volume of extra water would soon rise so high that it would cover the land and before long all the people and their animals would be swept away. And now there was absolutely nothing we could do to help them, it was too late. Maybe if we had taken more notice of Father ourselves when he talked about the wrath of God, we would have been able to convince some of them at least to heed his warnings. Uncomfortable thoughts were starting to go round and round in our heads.

"Surely even this amount of rain won't actually float the ark?" said Japhet peering out of one of the windows. "Even if it continues for 40 days and 40 nights as Father said it would, it will take a while."

But, only a few hours later, far faster than we would ever have thought possible, instead of just swirling round us, the water level had risen so high that it started lapping against the sides of the ark.

With our limited knowledge and experience, there was no way we could know that the chaos being wreaked by the rain inland was now meeting the force of the waters of the far oceans, where great eruptions on the sea bed were releasing subterranean waters from below and flooding the land from all directions. This lethal combination raised the water level so high that it finally floated the ark right off the foothills where we had built it, just as Father had predicted that it would.

And as the water started to float the ark off the ground we were alarmed to feel it tilting right over, first to one side and then the other, as the enormous wooden struts that had been supporting it for so long finally collapsed and floated away, smashed out of place by the tremendous force of the water. Then we could hear and feel the bottom of the ark grinding along the ground and Father worried that some of the planks in the base might crack under the pressure created by the weight of the ark and spring a leak. We began to hit the higher ground sideways on with such thunderous jolts that it was hard to keep our feet and not panic. But, finally, the ominous rasping noises stopped and we began to float.

Nahlat, who could be so haughty and reserved, looked absolutely terrified most of the time and huddled against Ham for comfort whenever she could. I had never seen anyone sneeze or blow their nose so frequently. Arisisah, who had disappeared for a while, was her usual quiet self on her return and I noticed that she seemed to be comforting Japhet, rather than the other way round. I was proud that Salit remained calm for most of the time and I found it a great comfort to put my arm round her shoulder protectively. In our own way each of us helped each other to remain strong. Mother and Father spent a lot of time in our living quarters, where Father was probably praying; at least we all hoped he was. It was a difficult and terrifying time for everything on the ark, man or beast.

A day or so later, although it was still raining, the storm had subsided a little and Father went out on deck for some air. He returned ashen-faced and soaking wet.

"Have you been outside, Father?" asked Japhet, rather unnecessarily I remember thinking, as Father stood there with the rain dripping off him and puddling at his feet.

"I have and I wish with all my heart I had not."

"Why?" asked Ham immediately. "What is it?"

"Even you would not want to know," Father replied.

But of course we were all dying to know what had shocked him so much, even if it was something as terrible as Father had intimated that it was. But we couldn't go up on deck immediately as that would have looked as if we were blatantly ignoring his warning.

"But he only said he wished he had not," reasoned Japhet, "so, that means that we can go if we want to, surely?"

So Ham, Shem and I sidled away out of sight to the nearest ladder and climbed out on deck, curious to see what had upset Father so much. There was another brief lull in the storm and the wind was lower than before. In the quiet between gusts, we could hear faint cries coming from below us.

"People," said Ham looking shocked.

"People," I echoed him. "Other people."

"Where are they, then?" asked Japhet, as if we would know.

"Shall I look over the side?" Ham asked us.

"No, don't," I said. "It will be a terrible sight, something you will never be able to get out of your mind, and there is nothing we can do. Let's just go back inside."

"And don't say anything about this, not just because we ignored Father's advice, but because it would upset all the women terribly to hear of it," said Japhet wisely.

"But what I don't understand is how can anybody possibly be alive after all this," said Ham.

"I don't know," I replied, "but it certainly sounded as if some of them were."

After that, none of us ever mentioned the incident again.

The rain kept on falling and the water level kept rising until the very last signs of land disappeared from sight. The summits of mountains, some of which protruded from the water long after we had floated away from our hillside, were finally submerged. And although we knew they were a potential danger, we could do nothing about it. We had no rudder to steer away from them, or to control our direction, which was nerve-wracking. And even when it appeared that all land had vanished from sight, there were still bits of debris of all shapes and sizes floating around the ark and constantly knocking into us. There was no way to avoid them and the potential damage they might have done to the ark, but eventually this happened less and less.

So we floated on over the vanishing world until one day Ham, who was braving the torrential rain out on deck, was astonished to see the peaks of a prominent mountain range ahead, still very visible above the water. In spite of the rain we rushed up on deck to see this unexpected sight. The mountains were quite close and even more surprisingly we thought we could see some movement on one of them. Sure enough, it was just possible to make out the shapes of several HUGE lizard-like creatures that were apparently trapped on the highest peak. As we floated towards them, we could hear them roaring and thrashing about as the floodwaters rose around them. There was a brief discussion as to what we should do, before Mother forcibly pointed out that they were so large that they would probably sink the ark and eat us all.

To Mother's irritation, Father appeared to be uncertain about what to do, but the matter was finally settled when he realised that there was no way of steering over to them without a rudder and the ark was floating past well out of their reach. Behind Father's back Ham gave us the thumbs up and the matter was dropped. But Mother was still so shaken that she didn't seem to realise the danger was past and continued to emphasise her point: "It's them or us, or rather me. I've put up with rats, snakes, toads, wasps, flies, tigers and pigs, but I absolutely draw the line at them, whatever they are," she exclaimed, gesticulating in their direction through the rain, but we had already floated on past and we soon lost sight of them altogether.

"Come, my dear," said Father guiding her back inside. "All of us agree, the danger is over now, you need to come in and change your robes, all of us are soaked through."

He was right, this happened whenever any of us went out on deck and this time the whole family was drenched. Inside the beams of the ark were soon festooned like an indoor market with our garments as they dried.

As we floated on and on in the pouring rain, we had no idea whether we were heading anywhere in particular, or simply going round in circles. Very occasionally we still collided with various bits of floating debris, but most of it was so waterlogged by now that it simply glanced off us with a dull thud. The constant rain obscured almost everything and it was if we were living in a perpetual half-light. There was no longer any real night or day, nor sunrise or sunset by which to get our bearings. And as we had no rudder, we could not steer in any particular direction; we were totally at the mercy of the elements.

Inside the ark we were already getting on each other's nerves.

"If Father says 'God is our rudder' once more I don't know what I'll do," said Ham.

"Push him overboard?" suggested Japhet. And I admit that there were times when I would gladly have helped him.

A few days, or maybe it was weeks, into the voyage and things inside the ark were not going particularly well. The weather had been too rough for any of us to go outside again and in spite of the ark's great size we all felt claustrophobic. With the planks of the deck constantly awash and treacherously slippery all the entrances had to be kept closed.

To make matters worse, most of the animals were still eating heartily and some of them were feeling the effects of the rough weather as well, many of them had diarrhoea and or vomiting which smelt appalling; even the birds on their roof perches seemed to be particularly prolific. As for us, every now and then one of us would disappear to be sick in some quiet corner. The pitch we had used for waterproofing the planks of the ark also exuded an unpleasantly strong odour, which I no longer found comforting as it added to the overpowering stench inside. All this had a particularly unfortunate effect on our wives, who spent as much time as they could lying prone on their beds, looking pale and sickly.

There were other problems. While we had carefully planned how we would feed the animals, in our ignorance we had never realised that they would need to be cleaned out so regularly. In our old life, when all the animals ran free most of the time, it had not been a consideration. But we soon realised that we couldn't just leave their droppings piling up in their stalls and the longer we left it, the worse it got. With the amounts involved, it rapidly became obvious that this was something we could not just ignore or argue about. It had to be dealt with on a much more frequent basis than we had anticipated, or we would soon have a serious problem.

"Things just get better and better, don't they?" muttered Ham.

"Oh, don't worry; it's all there, everything we need. Those chutes leading to the outside are not only to drain water off the different levels, they are for the droppings too," said Japhet proudly. "It's more work, yes, but we can't just leave it, can we?" Of course he was right. We couldn't. There was nothing for it but to drag the droppings from the stalls on jute sacks and shovel them out of the drainage chutes.

The chutes had to be used very carefully, which was difficult with such a large accumulation of waste. As the ark rolled up and down amongst the waves of the stormy sea, the shutter of the chute could only be opened safely when that side of the ark was high out of the water, or the ark would have flooded. It was all a bit of a nightmare at first. Timing was vital, as we didn't have long to shovel out as much as possible before the ark rolled and sank down into the water again.

Once the necessity for regular disposal was addressed, it was clear that it was going to be too much for the men to do alone. In spite of being unwell, our wives would simply have to clean out the smaller animals and birds, while Japhet did the medium-sized animals and Father and Ham and I cleaned out the largest. With the feeding of so many animals to be done as well we had an enormous amount of work to do every day.

There just weren't enough hours to do it in. And I for one began to pine for the time we spent in the clearing, when all we had to do was build the ark. As things were, we were constantly exhausted;

it was an absolutely awful time. And when I thought of the 40 days and 40 nights of this that Father had foretold I almost cried out loud with misery.

God's Rules

Unfortunately, even after the flood, God's plan to start afresh failed to bring a permanent end to the bad behaviour of man. So, having promised Noah that there would be no more apocalyptic floods, many years later in an attempt to modify his people's behaviour, God gave Moses, who led the Israelites out of Egypt and away from their life of slavery, a set of rules to live by known as the Ten Commandments. The future wellbeing of the Israelites was to be conditional on their adherence to those Ten Commandments of the Mosaic Covenant.

These declared that they were to have no other gods than God, not make idols, nor take God's name in vain. They were to honour their Mother and their Father and keep the Sabbath. They were not to murder, commit adultery, steal, bear false witness or covet.

Whilst there are no specific details of all the things that angered God so much that he decided to flood the earth hundreds of years before the birth of Moses, presumably the Ten Commandments give a strong indication of the behaviour that particularly annoyed him when he saw it continuing even after the flood.

⊙∽♠∾⊙

Chapter 11

⬥

L ife on board the ark could not have been more different from the life we had lived before. We were country people used to having our feet on the ground and living our lives according to the aspects of the sun and the moon, the seasons of the year and the needs of our animals and crops, to say nothing of the foibles and demands of the village priests. So it took us a quite a while to accustom ourselves to living within the confines of the ark, answerable only to ourselves. Shut in day and night, with hundreds of animals and birds, while storms constantly rocked and buffeted us, took some getting used to. Everything that needed to be done, we had to do ourselves and we learned by bitter experience that the longer we tried to avoid some of the less pleasant chores, the worse things became.

At the beginning of the voyage our days started early with a noisy and prolonged performance of the dawn chorus, as the hundreds of birds in the roof above us tuned in song by song. Fortunately it wasn't long before the birds no longer seemed to be able to tell when the dawn was without being able to see the sun appearing on the horizon in the morning. Gradually, day-by-day, the early morning cacophony dwindled with the exception of the odd cheep here and there, until it became virtually non-existent. Perversely, when it finally stopped, instead of feeling unmitigated relief, we rather missed it and it added to an unutterable sadness at yet another loss of something from our old familiar way of life.

One bird stubbornly continued to crow: the cockerel. Without the dawn to help him gauge the start of the day, his time-keeping was very erratic but, to give him his due, he always tried. Once the crowing had finished, Ham made his first remark of the day and it was always the same: "That cockerel would make a fine stew."

"Well, we have to get up some time," said Japhet.

"But does it always have to be so early?" Ham moaned.

"So what time is it, then?" asked Japhet.

"Well of course I don't know exactly what time it is, it just feels too early," replied Ham.

"If we don't start work soon, we'll never get it all done," I said. "And if we start any later we'll never have any time to ourselves."

"That's very true," said Ham glumly. "Nahlat says much the same, when she's not sneezing, or complaining about something else."

With so much to do we soon fell into a daily routine. First of all we fed the animals, starting as early as possible, which gave us time to do our other tasks as well. The grain eaters always seemed to be the most anxious to be fed, so Japhet shot their feed down the chutes from the middle deck to the main collection points and then we all pulled wooden sleds laden with buckets of feed along the rows of animals, tipping the grain into their food containers. The next to be fed were the hay eaters and finally the carnivores whose diet consisted of livid-looking strips of dry meat that they gnawed at for hours on end. This didn't surprise me, as the small amounts of dried meat that we ate had to be soaked for days in some kind of spicy liquid to tenderise it, or we wouldn't have finished chewing it from one meal to the next. While Mother said it was good for us, I think the rest of us found it pretty disgusting and Ham's comments about it were unrepeatable.

The drinking water came down from huge tanks on the roof to large containers inside the ark, two on every level. We watered the animals last, so that the dust from the hay and grains didn't blow into the drinking troughs any more than could be helped. Often we would find something swimming in one or more of the troughs, desperately trying to get out. I wondered, will they never learn?

Quite often I was woken first thing in the morning even before the cockerel crowed and well before I would have chosen to get up.

113

There would be a small splash in the nearest trough as something popped in for an early morning dip. Then, knowing what would happen next, I would wait, wide awake by then, alert for the sounds of anxious scrabbling to start, which meant that I had to get up and fish the panicking swimmer out of the water to safety. "Absolutely no common sense," I'd grumble to myself, as I returned to my bed where I would toss and turn with irritation as I tried to get back to sleep.

Our wives started their day a little later than us men, rising when the hungry cries, grunts and snuffles from the middle-deck animals whose pens surrounded our living quarters became too loudly insistent for them to ignore. Salit, Arisisah and Nahlat did most of the feeding, while Mother made our morning meal and catered for any of the animals needing special food. She and Arisisah also tended to any of the animals that had injuries or were sickly, which was vitally important, as we could not afford to lose any of them.

The easiest of all to feed were the birds, which ate relatively little, in spite of there being so many of them. We had constructed a constant feeding contraption that ran the length of the perches, as most of them liked to feed little and often. Unfortunately this fuelled a constant supply of bird droppings and seed husks that dropped down on us from above, but it couldn't be helped.

One thing we were never short of was eggs; there were eggs of every description, which we either ate ourselves or used to supplement the diets of some of the other animals. We became egg experts and could usually distinguish one from the other quite easily. For some odd reason, Father was an absolute champion at this. "A dodo if I'm not mistaken," he'd say, looking at the large chalky egg in his bowl, "I really can't eat all this by myself, thank you Mother."

"Of course there will come a time," said Japhet "when we have to stop eating all these eggs and allow some of them to hatch, especially those of birds like the dodo that only occasionally laid one large egg."

114

The rest of us groaned with mock dismay, but we knew he was right.

"Maybe we can do that when we are able to fish," said Father. He did not elaborate on when that might be, but it was yet another example of him appearing to know things that the rest of us could see no explanation for, and he was always right, or so it seemed.

Fortunately for all of us, the binding property of all these eggs was counteracted by our daily treat of dried figs and dates. Too many of these could of course be a great deal more effective than was required as Japhet, who had a very sweet tooth, could verify.

I liked figs and dates well enough, but they did get a little boring day after day and sometimes my attention turned to the reed beehive that we had secured to a pole near Father's vines in the hold of the ark. It hadn't been at all easy to get the bees into the reed basket and then they swarmed just before the rain came, which had been a nuisance and a worry when we had so many other things to do. So now we had no idea exactly how many bees there were left in it. We knew it was not nearly as many as before, but certainly a great many more than seven. Not, I might add, that anyone had ever suggested eating or sacrificing any of the extra ones or trying to count them for that matter.

With no pollen-bearing blossoms on board, the bees were unable to make any more honey and quickly retired into the hive to survive on their stores. And the thought of all this honey really played on my mind. There were times when I had an almost irresistible urge to open the hive for just a tiny taste, which would probably have infuriated the bees. But every time I was tempted, someone would start calling for help, or be too close to the hive for me to get away with raiding it without being seen. Strangely I never considered the risk of being stung, so overwhelming was my desire for the sticky sweetness of the honey.

Naturally things didn't always go smoothly and we had numerous unexpected problems. Our main concern was that once the animals had settled in to life on the ark some of them seemed to have developed extraordinarily voracious appetites, eating far more than we had ever expected them to. This was worrying because we hadn't taken this into account when calculating what supplies we would need. With the exception of the bears, it didn't seem to be anything to do with size, but it was very obvious that a significant proportion of the animals were consuming an extraordinary amount of food.

"If they all go on eating at this rate, Father," said Japhet, "the food supplies will run out long before the voyage is over," not that he actually knew how long that would be. "They even seem to be getting noticeably fatter and of course they have no opportunity to exercise at the moment, so that doesn't help."

"Don't worry, Japhet, everything will be fine; God will provide," said Father.

Japhet, who had overall responsibility for the food supplies, was obviously not totally convinced, but unlike Ham who would have argued with Father he held his tongue.

And once again, Father was to be proved right.

Even with the enormous number of animals that had to be fed, the huge amount of food we had stored on board at the start of the voyage had seemed to be excessive. We had wondered how we could possibly need it all, and yet here we were, having pretty much lost track of time, with no idea how much longer our supplies would need to last, already anxiously wondering whether we would have enough. And then, if we didn't have enough, what would we do? The animals would starve.

There were only two options that we could see, either the food would have to miraculously increase, or the number of animals needing to be fed would have to decrease. But for the life of us we couldn't see how either of these alternatives would come about. As always, Father was irrationally optimistic that everything would work out.

The first clues we had that something unusual was happening were changes in the animals' daily routine. Normally some of them woke up early and some of them late, but now a fair number of them appeared to be constantly drowsy and then they began to sleep nearly all the time, hardly waking up at all. At first we were worried that we were doing something wrong. Was it was our fault, were these animals ill or were they sickening for something? What on earth was wrong with them all? We even thought that some of them were dead, but when we knelt down beside them and listened carefully they were still breathing. We drew straws as to who should listen to see if the bears were still breathing...

"But of course," Japhet shouted one day, "I've got it. I think I know exactly what's going on here; they're not ill, this behaviour is quite natural and logical. They are hibernating. Why didn't I think of it before?"

I wondered what on earth he was talking about.

"That's why they were all eating so much food; they were building up their strength to keep them going while they sleep," he explained.

"And how long does this sleeping go on?" I asked.

"For months usually," replied Japhet.

"Wonderful!" Ham shouted out delightedly. "No more feeding them then and, even better, no more mucking them out! Do elephants or pandas hibernate by any chance?"

"Or bison or giraffes, rhinoceros, hippos or zebras?" I asked hopefully.

Unfortunately as it turned out, they do not. But there was more good news from Japhet. "Not only do some animals hibernate in the cold of the winter," he said, "other animals do something similar to hibernation in very hot conditions so, as it's pretty warm on board, especially on the middle deck, we may get some of them dropping off as well."

We all hoped that he was right.

The largest of all the animals to hibernate were the bears, so we had to be grateful for that. For some reason Japhet seemed very relieved that the skunks hibernated too, but he was a bit mysterious about why. He just smiled and said, "You'll probably see why one day," in an irritating way.

Most of the other hibernating animals were quite small: hedgehogs, squirrels, chipmunks, gophers, bats and snakes all fell asleep gradually, over the first few weeks of the voyage. I remember being particularly relieved when the last of the snakes to stay awake finally stopped gliding about and curled up amongst the stones in their compartments before nodding off.

In spite of the hibernating animals taking some of the pressure off us we still had more than enough work to do and by far the worst and most unpopular task was the daily cleaning out of the stalls and pens. We no longer mucked out all the stalls every day, but it still took the three of us most of the morning to finish them once we had done the feeding. The trouble was that virtually none of the large animals slept and we needed to clean them out regularly, or the smell inside the ark, which was already just this side of overpowering, would have become unbearable.

Although it was cold outside and the rain fell incessantly, the inside of the ark was warm. We still had to keep the shutters shut all the time, though, which made it depressingly gloomy day after day. It didn't help that once we had the animals on board, we had had to cut down on the number of candles and oil lamps we lit, in case they got knocked over and started a fire. The temperature and dim conditions did provide one great advantage, though, by keeping all the animals that were still awake fairly calm. And as they had little or no activity, even the animals not actually hibernating became lethargic and ate less and less as time went on. With the amount of work we still had to do every day, I could have eaten a goat for every meal and I often looked enviously at the animals that spent the day quietly dozing in their stalls.

After we had fed all the animals that were still awake, Father led us in prayer for the day ahead and then we had a meal, a short rest and a daily discussion, to decide what needed doing and, more importantly, which one of us would do it. All around us we could hear the comforting sound of animals gently chewing their food, while a light rain of seed husks floated down from the rafters and branches above us. The rush matting was very effective at shielding us from their droppings, but unfortunately the seed husks

118

easily permeated it. At first Mother insisted that these were regularly swept up, but when she realised that they actually made a pleasant soft surface to walk on, we were allowed to let them accumulate in the passages, where they had the added benefit of muffling the noise.

Our living quarters were very plain; the roof and walls were made of heavy matting, bare of any decoration apart from some ornate robes, which belonged to Nahlat hanging on one wall. The floor was covered with rush mats and we slept on an assortment of cushions and mattresses that were also used on the seats round the communal table in the daytime. Only Mother and Father had a curtain hanging which could be drawn across to separate them from the rest of us, but they seldom bothered to use it.

In the daytime we were rarely there together apart from mealtimes and at night all any of us wanted to do was sleep.

Any personal treasures that we had managed to bring with us were stored in a few baskets and pots hanging from the walls, most of which had been commandeered by Nahlat.

On either side of our quarters we housed some of the friendlier small animals and behind us there was a wall of dry food supplies, which had the benefit of keeping us warm as well as smelling homely and comforting. We had learned to ignore the rustling and nibbling sounds of the mice and rats. 'Rats' was a word that was never mentioned in front of our wives, or they might have insisted on us trying to hunt them down, or even moving our sleeping quarters. However, we had all been through so much by then, that I think everyone's sensibilities about such things were less honed than they had been.

Our meals were cooked on a fire that was laid in a large metal bowl and we ate from clay dishes, which regularly slid from the table and crashed to the floor, where the spilt food was immediately gulped down by the ever-watchful cats and dogs. In the evening they usually joined us round the fire, lying quietly at our feet, but if there was any trouble at all amongst them, Ham ruthlessly put them all out in the passage.

119

Most of the other animals had to be kept contained in their stalls for safety, but that didn't stop some of them taking a great interest in the aroma of the food that Mother and Salit cooked for us. Arisisah was in charge of adding herbs and flavouring, to vary the taste of the limited ingredients that we had on board. I was always so hungry at mealtimes that I could have eaten almost anything, but I had been married long enough by now to know that this would not have been regarded, by any of the cooks, as a complimentary remark, so nothing much was said bar the odd grunt of approval as our bellies filled.

As the days and then the weeks went by, the stuffy atmosphere and monotony of our existence had an increasingly stupefying affect on everyone, not just the animals. By now, there were times when the only sign of life inside the ark was when some of the smaller animals amused themselves by racing round their enclosures in sudden mad bursts of energy. Even the birds had become quieter and less active; lethargy seemed to have overcome us all. And none of us was particularly interested in time passing any more or worrying about things we could do nothing about. We only had enough energy to do the things we absolutely had to do to survive.

What Could Have Caused the Flood?

———————

Of course the answer that immediately springs to mind is the 40 days and 40 nights of rain described in Genesis as falling from the "windows of heaven" having a cumulative effect and causing rivers, streams, lakes and pools to overflow and the level of the sea to rise.

Genesis also describes the "fountains of the deep" being in turmoil, which could have referred to movement along the fault lines in the earth's tectonic plates, the sheets of basalt and granite five to 30 miles thick that form the crust of the earth below the land and sea.

The plates of the earth's crust float on viscous, semi-molten rocks (the earth's mantle) and it is not unusual for them to move a few inches a year, propelled by currents in the molten mantle. Where the plates are pushed apart, the lava (molten rock) may well up from below and cause volcanic eruption and earthquakes. When the plates do not slide smoothly but catch, they can jolt feet apart in an instant causing earthquakes and, due to a massive displacement of water at sea, the disastrous phenomenon, the tsunami.

❦

Chapter 12

◁◇▷

One of the things Father made very clear to us all right from the start was that he never wanted to hear us discussing our old life; in fact he forbade us to do so. This was undoubtedly to try and keep our spirits up, but it was easy to get round this by waiting until he was not about. We couldn't help dwelling on our neighbours' fate and what must have happened to them. Although Ham, Japhet and I did not have any particularly close friends outside the family, there were neighbours who in spite of everything we had liked and remembered fondly. These were people who we had sometimes helped and who had helped us in return, even if our relationships had changed once we started building the ark.

"I don't know what they'll all do without you around to help them," Ham said to me one day without thinking. Then realising what he had said, he bowed his head in awkward embarrassment. For once, there was no humour to be had from his observation and as he turned away from me I saw that tears had welled up in his eyes. However unpleasant things had got over the ark, it was hard not to remember some of the good times and none of us would have wished the terrible fate that became of our village on even the most unpleasant of our old neighbours.

Our wives had some close friends amongst the other women of the village. Salit had grown up there and, through her, Nahlat and Arisisah had got to know nearly everyone. All the women tended to be more understanding of husbandly foibles, even ones as extreme as building an ark and so, right up until our final departure from the village, the village women almost all remained on civil terms. The wives were more wary of openly defying Father and talking about the old days, but I am sure they did and when their feelings became too much for them, one or other of them would rush away from the rest of us in tears. I couldn't help thinking how odd it was that we seemed to remember more about the good times before we started building the ark and less about the difficulties and ridicule we faced during its building.

It was an awkward situation and all of us understood why Father wanted to try and spare us the pain of confronting it. However, no one can control their thoughts and feelings entirely no matter how hard they try. When I really needed to get a grip on my emotions I tried to concentrate on how unpleasant some of the people had been to us while we were building the ark, but even then it was hard.

Our grandfather Lamech was another fertile topic of conversation, but we naturally talked of him with great respect, especially in front of Father. He died before the ark was completed and it makes me smile to remember how difficult he found it to try and understand what his son was doing and why. His life had not been without controversy, even if it had not featured anything on the scale of building an ark. We all remembered him fondly and the fact that some people regarded his life as unconventional did nothing to change this. From our earliest boyhood he had been a mine of information and wisdom. He was not as serious as Father, in fact with us boys he was not serious at all, and we had all loved listening to his stories.

While at this stage life inside the ark was mostly rather dull, conditions outside were still far from tranquil. The rain poured down relentlessly, drumming on the outside of the ark and intermittent flashes of lightning still ripped across the sky, followed by rumbles of thunder so loud that they seemed to be the very embodiment of God's anger with man and we were all terrified. Sometimes the ark rocked so violently in the water that we all instinctively braced ourselves, in case we had hit something but, apart from the odd bits of floating detritus, there seemed little chance of hitting anything. We were so far adrift by now that all the land that we had once known must have disappeared far below the surface of the water. Sometimes we heard far away sounds, like great doors slamming underwater or subterranean explosions, and it felt as if the water was boiling beneath us as the ark was buffeted violently by the aftershock. We had no means of steering and no idea where we were, and I am sure that at such times even Father's trust in God must have been put to the test.

Sometimes, the clash of elements around the ark alarmed us so much that we all panicked, including the animals and birds, and then there was total pandemonium on board. The larger animals plunged around their stalls and the smaller ones squeaked and moaned in fear, burrowing and scrabbling, trying to hide away in the corners of their pens. The birds would take off from their perches en masse and later, when things had quietened down again, we would find them hiding away in nooks and crannies all over the ark.

With no means of steering or steadying ourselves whatsoever, we were totally at the mercy of the elements. The sky remained overcast and the rain constant and heavy; there was virtually no change between day and night and no way of gauging our whereabouts, or in which direction we were travelling.

"We are all absolutely helpless you know," pronounced Japhet, after another particularly unpleasant episode. "There is absolutely nothing we can do to help ourselves."

"Oh do shut up Japhet," I said. "Somehow, it just doesn't help to hear you put it into words."

"All right you two," said Ham, "to be honest it really wouldn't help us at all if we did have sails or a rudder. We still wouldn't know what to do with them, so does it really matter?"

I had to admit that he had a point, but then we had never built a boat before and look what we had managed to do.

"Well, God really will have to be our rudder then," said Japhet innocently.

Ham and I were not amused.

Now there was less to do, we passed some of our time watching the animals that were still awake and, of course, there was a huge variety of them to choose from. Most of their needs such as their preferred food we could work out just by observing them and using our common sense. At the beginning we made mistakes all the time, giving dried meat to herbivores and grains to meat eaters, who regarded their new and unsuitable diet with an understandable lack of enthusiasm or even alarm. Japhet would say, "Look at their teeth... sharp, pointed teeth means meat, blunt teeth means grass or grains." But as they were not in their normal habitat it was difficult to tell if they were behaving normally or not.

Some things were obvious. It didn't take us long to work out that the dodos were amongst the most foolish creatures on board. The large, portly birds with jaunty tails that looked as if they had been stuck on as an afterthought, short stubby wings and large beaks, couldn't fly and had an infallible knack for being in the wrong place at the wrong time. It was a miracle that they weren't squashed or trodden on even more often than they were. Nothing seemed to keep them in their pen and, having escaped, they would proceed at a stately pace down the centre of the passage where they invariably got in someone's way. If anything excited them they stood and flapped their inadequate wings, which got them nowhere, and if they were cornered they were capable of giving a nasty peck, but their ridiculous appearance was still rather endearing. Almost every day someone would remark, "If both those birds survive the voyage it will be a miracle". I thought it was already miracle that two of them had survived long enough to get onto the ark in the first place.

Then there were the lemmings, although Ham had some rather more colourful names for them. I am sure we only had two when we started and there was no reason to let more than two on board as they certainly weren't sacrifice material. But it wasn't long before there were many, many more of them all running about together in a strangely cohesive formation, getting in everyone's way.

"If it's not the blasted dodos, it's those damned lemmings,"

125

Ham would rant as a stream of small brown animals flowed down one of the passageways in front of him.

"I don't mind them actually," said Japhet. "They rather remind me of our old sheep flock." At which Ham rolled his eyes.

All the black and white animals and the magpies were in a category of their own. Ham was right: they really did seem to be more difficult and cantankerous than the rest of the animals. The pandas refused to cohabit, were fussy but voracious eaters and produced prodigious amounts of droppings. The zebras were extremely unfriendly and bad-tempered and no one liked going into their pen. The magpies were annoying, with harsh cries and thieving proclivities, and even the beautiful black and white lemurs were depressing to look after, looking at us mournfully with their large yellow eyes and their tails wrapped tightly round the poles in their stall.

"I think they're missing the sun," said Japhet speculatively.

And they weren't the only ones.

The lemmings were not the only fast breeders, there were many others as well. There were times when the middle deck seemed to be alive with carpets of rabbits, lemmings and mice and there seemed to be quite a few kittens about as well. The best method of getting them out of the way was to bang the side of the gangway with a brush or a stick and then they would all vanish as if by magic.

Then there was the opposite extreme such as the pandas that, in spite of all our endeavours, steadfastly refused to go near each other. Neither would leave their pen if they could help it and neither of them would ever go into each other's quarters; they had clearly taken a great dislike to one another.

"It really is most unfortunate," Father said.

"Terminal I should say," said Ham.

"Give them time," said Japhet, optimistically.

"It's a shame really, they're actually one of the nicer black and white species," said Ham. "Maybe we just chose the wrong pair? Or maybe they're both the same sex?"

"Well I don't think there were any others, just those two that I saw. I'm absolutely sure of it," said Japhet.

Animals such as the sheep, goats and cows had come on board in sevens, according to God's command. These were the animals that we were permitted to eat and that were also acceptable as sacrificial offerings. But, for the sake of harmony and a certain amount of diplomacy, it was unanimously – if reluctantly – agreed that we would not kill and eat any of the animals during the voyage. We had not decided what to do if any of the edible ones died, but obviously the smell of their fellow passengers being cooked would hardly have promoted a feeling of wellbeing amongst the rest of them. We did have the dried meat strips, which Mother and Arisisah used to cook stews, but the pungent smell of herbs masked any meaty aroma (and most of the taste), unlike fire-roasted fresh meat. These stews never tasted particularly good and when the dried meat finally ran out none of us cared very much.

Sadly there were some casualties quite early on, which was upsetting and, more seriously, signified the end for that particular species. One of the first victims was one of the flats. Not the most attractive of animals, flat by name and appearance, with not much fur and small feet at each corner that it used to scrabble along in a very awkward manner.

Ham dangled the poor dead creature in front of us by a foot...

"How on earth did this happen?" asked Japhet. "Father will be furious."

"Possibly trodden on?" said Ham, without going into any further details.

With so many animals on board, there were escapes and disappearances almost daily but, as long as the escapee was not dangerous, we didn't worry too much. We always knew for certain that it must be on the ark somewhere and that it would turn up in the end. Much more serious were the occasional casualties like the flat, which must have slid beneath the door of its cage and out into the danger of the open corridors, or into a neighbouring stall, where something had unwittingly squashed it.

Then one word immediately came to mind: extinction.

Animals with the ability to camouflage themselves also caused a certain amount anxiety, especially at the beginning of the voyage before we became more relaxed about everything. Mother's eyesight wasn't what it had been and although she was always reporting animals missing, her worries could usually be taken with a pinch of salt. The chameleons were obviously hard to see, but when she wandered down to the lower deck she sometimes failed to make out animals like the cheetahs and even the tigers that tended to melt into the background of straw in their stalls. So, in spite of her anxiety, we became used to these false alarms and learned to assess the reliability of her fears on the missing animal's ability to disguise itself before we started to panic.

Some of the animals did not really need their own living quarters. The cats curled up in the warm wherever they pleased and the dogs lay around wherever it suited them. They liked human company and usually followed one or other of us around for most of the day.

Their empty stalls were useful if any of the other animals became unwell and needed some peace and quiet. There was no way we could contain animals like the mice and the rats, who were consummate escape artists, so we didn't even try and soon we estimated that there were more of them on board than most of the other animals put together. Fortunately they usually remained discreetly hidden, or the ark would have resounded with the terrified shrieks of our wives. Luckily the gestation periods of the larger animals were far longer, or things could have become rather difficult.

Amongst the strangest creatures on board were the yetis that had given us such a fright when they appeared at the top of the gangplank at the last minute and then just shot on board and disappeared. With so much else going on, those of us who had originally seen them soon forgot about them. They never seemed to appear for food or to drink as far as we could tell and with so many other distractions there was nothing to remind us of their presence until we actually saw them again. Japhet discovered them right up in the bows of the ark where it was the coldest, huddled up together in a pile of straw and goatskins.

"Aaagh, what are they? Who are they? What are they doing here?" Japhet shouted out, alarmed by his discovery.

"You remember them," I said. "They were nearly the last on board, Ham saw them too and so did Father, they looked really frightened of us and darted off once inside the ark, then they just disappeared and that was that."

"They look sleepy," said Ham peering over my shoulder to see what was going on. "Quite big, aren't they?"

"And they really do look quite like us and very like Japhet used to, when he'd been off with the sheep for a few months," said Arisisah, who had heard her husband's shouts.

"Oh all right, all right," he laughed, feeling more confident now that he was not alone with the yetis anymore. "So what are we going to do with them?"

"They look very sleepy," said Arisisah, "perhaps they would like some food and water after being disturbed."

But although we offered them various kinds of food they didn't seem all that interested and after nervously sipping some water, they huddled up in their bedding again and we left them to it.

"They've got a lot of hair, haven't they?" said Ham.

"Well I think they look like a mixture of a gorilla and an orang-utan with white hair," said Japhet, who always liked to have an opinion on things like this. Arisisah simply looked at him and smiled.

They were an odd couple, sort of like us, but not like us. It was hard to explain even to myself. "Now that we know where they are, we had better keep more of an eye on them and check them regularly to make sure they are all right," said Father.

Noah

Noah's genealogy is recorded in great detail in the Old Testament. He is said to be of the ninth generation in the line of Adam, descended from Adam's third and youngest son, Seth. Seth was born after Adam's oldest son Abel had killed his brother Cain in a fit of jealousy.

Noah's grandfather, Methuselah, is recorded as having lived for 969 years and his father, Lamech, presciently named his son Noah, as "one who would bring comfort and rest from God's curse on the land of Cain".

Sumerian historical texts record Noah's birthplace as the town of Shuruppak, in the lands of Sumer near the future location of the important city of Uruk, whose ruins are still visible today in the bleak desert landscape. The ruins of the city are dominated by the remains of the great ziggurat, built to honour the city's goddess Inanna (or Ishtar). Inanna was the most important female deity of ancient Mesopotamia, a goddess of love, fertility, war and political power.

In the Dead Sea Scrolls, the oldest known biblical manuscripts, discovered in 1946, there is a description of Noah as a child: "Flesh was white as snow and red as a rose; the hair was white like wool, and long; eyes were beautiful and when he opened them, he illuminated all the house, like the sun".

In the Bible it is said that Noah had three sons, Ham, Shem and Japhet. Islamic scholars believe Noah had four sons, the fourth being Yam, a disbeliever, who refused to board the ark. Instead, ignoring his father's warnings, he is said to have climbed a mountain and was drowned by the flood.

Prior to the flood Noah is recorded as being the only blameless and righteous man of his generation. And whilst his daughters in law are named in some accounts of the flood, his wife is not. Her biblical name, according to Muslim tradition, is Naamah, although there are scholars who assert her name was Umzrah bint Barakil.

In the Old Testament of the Bible, Noah was said to be 500 years old when he was told to build the ark. The construction took over 100 years to complete and after the flood he is said to have lived for a further 350 years – nearly as long as Methuselah.

☙❧

Chapter 13

As time went on, even more of the animals fell asleep or dozed most of the time, which meant that mucking out and feeding duties took up less and less of our day. And, with fewer chores to do and more time on our hands, Ham and I were both starting to get bored. Japhet, on the other hand, had always found it easy to while away his time by relaxing wherever and whenever he got the chance. By now all of us knew every corner of the ark from top to bottom. Nothing new or surprising ever seemed to happen and we were finding being confined harder and harder.

We amused ourselves by playing with the animals and teaching the parrots and mynah birds phrases such as "Where's land?" and "God knows", which shocked Mother and would have infuriated Father if he had heard us. We tried blowing Father's horn, which was difficult to master and which irritated him and startled the animals. Then we attempted to play the flute, which was easier, but we could soon tell that we would never be anything like as good at it as Japhet or Father were, so we gave that up as well. We played gambling games with pebbles and straws and sometimes even our chores for forfeits, which Father would have frowned on previously but by now even he didn't have the heart to forbid. But it still wasn't nearly enough to occupy our spare time. We were outdoor men, used to having the freedom to roam about, so being cooped up inside became more and more intolerable.

While the rain continued to fall outside, the heat and smells inside the ark, with its minimal ventilation, became more oppressive every day. The continual gloom of the interior was only pierced by the occasional flash of plumage, as one of the more brightly coloured birds flitted across the ark from perch to perch by the light of the remaining candles.

"How many days has it been now, do you think?" asked Ham, sounding like a petulant child.

"Thirty four," answered Arisisah surprisingly quickly.

While we men had quickly lost all sense of time, unknown to us our wives had methodically kept a count of the days, using the behaviour of the animals that were still awake to work out roughly how long we had been on the ark.

"Thirty four days in the near dark, in this smelly, boring boat with these damned animals and these stinking birds, with the rain beating down night and day. I don't think I can stand much more of it, I really can't," said Ham dramatically, smacking his forehead. "I've got to get out of here."

"But you can't go out," Arisisah cried. "There's nowhere for you to go and you could easily be washed overboard."

"The way I feel at the moment to be honest, I couldn't care less," retorted Ham. "I've had enough."

Being used to Ham and his jokes, I didn't take him all that seriously at first, but I soon realised that he really was distressed. Arisisah must have come to the same conclusion and she was looking anxiously at him when suddenly Ham leaped to his feet and started to run along one of the side passages at the top of the middle deck. At the first window he came to, he started to struggle with the ties that were keeping it lashed shut.

I can't imagine how he managed to untie the fastenings so quickly, but he did. The wind and rain caught the wooden shutter as it flew open and there was a mighty crash as it blew back and hit the side of the ark with a bang. Then almost as if he had been sucked out, Ham rapidly disappeared through the window and the animals in the nearby stalls shrank back from the invasive force of the wind and rain that he had unleashed into the tranquillity of the ark.

"Shem, Japhet, do something ... He'll be washed overboard! Where's Nahlat? Fetch her now, he'll listen to her, I know he will!" shrieked Arisisah.

I doubted her voice would be loud enough to penetrate the noise of the elements howling round the ark but, as I looked outside, open-mouthed with shock as torrents of rain poured in through the open window, Nahlat appeared. Initially she seemed not to know what she was looking at, but when Arisisah told her she started to scream. "Ham ... Ham ... come back, come back inside, please, please, come back!"

But of course there was no way he could have heard her.

Her imploring cries and the possibility that she might try to join him outside herself forced me to do something. If nothing else, I must stop the shutter banging and banging, or the wind would tear it off the side of the ark. But as I reached the window, the ark lurched to one side and I tripped over my robes and stumbled to the floor. The fall finally brought me to my senses and, grabbing the rope that had secured the window, I jumped outside, still holding on to it as I landed on the treacherously slippery deck. Ham was nowhere to be seen, not that I could actually see very far through the sheets of rain. Waves of water continuously washed over the whole length of the deck and within seconds I was drenched. What a situation to be in, I thought, and I knew that I had to keep a firm hold of something to prevent myself being swept along the deck by the swirling water.

By now I was nearer to the front of the ark than the back, but I could see that Ham definitely wasn't there, so he must have gone towards the stern. I held on tight to the rope for as long as I could, but there was no sign of him and to move any further back I just had to let it go. All I could do then was to cling to anything that I could grab hold of along the side of the ark and cautiously make my way backwards. I was truly terrified that at any moment I could slip and be washed down the deck and overboard. Then, maybe it was my imagination or perhaps I was getting used to the situation, the waves seemed to calm down a little and the rain did not seem quite so fierce. But I still couldn't see any sign of Ham.

As I cautiously crept along the side of the ark I thought I heard a cry. I looked around but the visibility was so poor that I could see

134

nothing either ahead of me or behind. Then I definitely heard the voice cry out again, only just perceptible above the sounds of the waves and the rain.

"Shem! Shem!"

I peered backwards and forwards through the rain but I still couldn't see any sign of him. Then I heard my name being called again and I realised that the sound was coming from above me. Looking up, I saw Ham sitting astride the roof, holding on fast to one of the air vents. He was soaked but had a look of calm about him and he gestured to me to come up and join him. I wasn't so sure about this as the roof looked treacherously slippery, but I was so relieved to see him safe, that I decided to give it a go. At that very moment there was a tremendous bang behind me as the shutter of the ark slammed open again and Japhet's head popped out, looking around until he caught sight of us both. I yelled and gestured to him that we were safe and his head disappeared back inside again.

Luckily it was not such a difficult climb as I had first thought and with Ham's help I managed to scramble up the roof to where he was perched. And once I had finally clambered up onto the ridge beside him, he hugged me tight.

"Sorry Shem, I'm sorry, really sorry, I don't know what came over me but I just had to get out, it was just so claustrophobic in there I couldn't bear it for another minute more."

"I can see what you mean," I said, wiping rain from my eyes, while clutching tightly onto the air vent. "It's so much nicer out here, isn't it?"

"Well actually, in some ways it really is," he shouted above the wind and rain. "I just had to have a break away from it all – Father, the animals and Nahlat – just for a while at least, but there didn't seem to be a simple way to do it. I didn't mean to cause a scene."

"Well what did you expect?" I asked him. Now my relief was turning to anger. "Everyone else manages to cope, we're all tired of being cooped up inside. You're not the only one, you know."

"I know, I know," he replied. "I'm sorry; it's just the noise and the smell and the animals and Father. It's so hard with him being there all the time, making sure we do the right thing and always so certain he is right, however outrageous his demands and beliefs are."

"It must have been difficult for him as well," I shouted back. "It's a huge act of faith for him getting the ark built; think what he's done while all that time he was being mocked and jeered for his predictions."

"We were, too!" retorted Ham. "He couldn't have done much without us."

"But he was right, wasn't he? There was a flood and the animals did come just like he said and only we can possibly have survived."

At this Ham, who was clearly overwrought, broke down and wept, his tears mingling with the rain streaming down his face.

"But why did I survive?" he asked me, as if I knew the answer to this any more than he did. "I wasn't good, I wasn't better than anyone else, and I don't deserve to live, no more than lots of other people, anyway."

I had asked myself the same question many times. Why us? And all I could come up with was that we were the children of Noah, who was a uniquely good man, or as good a man as God could find at the time. We were his family and, for that reason only, we had been chosen to carry on the human race after the flood. I couldn't think of any other explanation.

Now I felt ashamed. How could I have been so arrogant as to think that it was only me who had found this a difficult idea to come to terms with? How could it possibly be fair? Frankly, as the thinker in the family, I would have thought Japhet would have been more concerned about this sort of thing. Instead, here I was, sitting on the roof of the ark in the torrential rain with Ham, who had always seemed to be the least reflective member of the family, while Japhet dozed inside. And now it seemed that it was Ham and not Japhet who was finding it the hardest to cope with all the consequences of the flood. But then how could we know what

Japhet really thought about it? We hadn't actually asked him and he had not had occasion to tell us. Mind you, a lot of discontented muttering went on amongst all of us.

And at that very moment, as we both sat on the ridge of the roof in the rain, the window below us banged open again and Japhet himself climbed out rather awkwardly and slithered down onto the deck. Unfortunately one of the parrots flew out behind him and, with a sickening squawk, blew away over the side of the ark.

Extinction.

"Can I come up there, too?" shouted Japhet, looking up at us from the deck.

"Why?" Ham shouted down, before I could stop him. "Have you got a message from Father?"

"No I haven't got a message from anyone; I just need to get outside as well. To have a break, you know."

"Well come on up then," yelled Ham, in as cordial a manner as he could manage, reaching down for him.

Having scrambled up beside us, Japhet steadied himself and grinned. "Whew, I really needed this, just to get outside; I don't know how we've coped for so long. Do you know how long it's been by the way?"

"Thirty four days," said Ham and I in unison.

"Well it feels like that many months," groaned Japhet. "Still, that means only six more days to go."

"Six more days to what?" asked Ham cautiously.

"Six more days of rain," replied Japhet. "According to Father."

"Oh yes, of course, that's if he's right," said Ham.

"He does seem to be doing quite well at being right so far," said Japhet.

I looked questioningly at them both, wondering what the hell they were talking about. Then it dawned on me: 40 days and 40 nights of rain had been foretold. The thought that the end could be in sight made me feel quite sick with relief.

"So, then what happens?" asked Ham. "Does the water just

vanish? And, if not, where will it all go and, most important of all, what will happen to us?"

"As I understand it, nothing dramatic will happen immediately the rain ceases," said Japhet. "It will just seep away, I suppose."

"Well how long will it take to seep?" asked Ham.

"That I don't know," replied Japhet, "you'll have to ask Father for the details."

Ham rolled his eyes at that and the three of us went on staring out from the roof for a while, saying nothing. We were a very bedraggled trio with our hair and clothes plastered to us, but all of us were glad to be outside even in such awful conditions.

Finally, of course, we had to get down off the ridge and make our way back inside. Ham volunteered to go first, whooping as he slid down the boards of the roof.

"You'd better watch out, Japhet, come down very slowly, or you'll hit the deck so fast that you might bounce right over the side."

"WHAT?" shouted Japhet, the wind was getting up again and Ham's words had blown away unheard.

"Oh, never mind," shouted Ham. "BE CAREFUL or Arisisah will never forgive me."

And with that Japhet slid down the roof at some speed, landing with a small splash as his sandals slapped down onto the wet deck.

Just for that moment, when the others had gone down, I was left alone up on the ridge of the roof and I felt as if I was sitting on top of the world; it was awe-inspiring. But as the rain poured down and the wind gusted all around me, my elation drained away and I suddenly felt like the loneliest man in the universe.

I thought for the umpteenth time what it must have been like for all those men, women and children who had perished. Rain, rain and more rain had fallen, and it wouldn't have been long before they must have realised that the level of the water was going to continue to rise and it wasn't going to drain away... that there wasn't anywhere for it to go and that there was no escape for them. Then I thought, suppose it doesn't go away for us either? Maybe we were simply deluding ourselves that we were special, and in the end we too would simply float away to a final watery death. Or perhaps Father's God, our God, would change his mind? Tears of sadness mixed with fear, self-pity and rain ran down my face until I couldn't see anything at all, let alone what the future might hold for us.

"ARE YOU GOING TO STAY UP THERE ON THE ROOF FOREVER?" Ham yelled up at me. "WE CAN'T GO IN WITHOUT YOU."

"I'M COMING!" I yelled down at him, wiping my eyes on my sodden sleeve before swinging my leg over the ridge and starting to slide. Unfortunately, almost at once, my robes caught on a splinter of wood, which ripped them right off my back and I landed on the deck naked, wearing just my sandals, while my waterlogged robes flapped limply from the roof above me. Then my tears of sadness turned to tears of laughter as I staggered to my feet. I made a feeble effort to climb back up for them, but Ham and Japhet grabbed hold of me and dragged me back down. Then all three of us, laughing hysterically, slipping and sliding, made our way back along the deck towards the window.

Ham and Japhet both scrambled back inside relatively easily, but as the last one outside and with no one left to help me I found it a great deal harder to get back into the ark. I also had to keep hold of the shutter as it was caught by gusts of wind so strong that they almost jerked my arms out of their sockets as I struggled to fasten it shut again. There was also the small matter of my nakedness. Unfortunately by this time absolutely everyone seemed to have gathered at the window, all of them waiting anxiously for the three of us to get back safely inside the ark again. The soaking wet figures of Ham and Japhet had created enough of a sensation, until I arrived. Mother looked shocked, Father looked on disapprovingly and I felt embarrassed. Arisisah, bless her, looked at me and began to laugh. And, thank God, with that everyone else started laughing as well. Cold, bedraggled and naked though I was the warmth of the ark and the sound of everyone laughing made me feel far better about everything than I had done for a very long time.

The warm and enthusiastic welcome my brothers and I received was far greater than we could have hoped for. There was no interrogation or recrimination, only joy and relief that all three of us were safely back inside. Salit was a little sharp with me later, but I knew it was only because she had been worried about me.

Our escapade had reminded everyone how long we had been on board and how long it had been since any of us had seen land or the sun, or even been outside. It had also drawn everyone's attention to the imminent end of the rainfall if things went according to plan. The prospect of an end to the rain made everyone feel more optimistic about our future.

Of course, as is the way of things, the final six days seemed to go by unbelievably slowly; we had all begun to count now, so there was absolutely no chance of us forgetting the allotted day. We tried to remember exactly when the rain had first started, and at exactly what time of day. We knew it had been light because I could remember running around the ark looking for things we had left lying around. Everyone seemed to have an odd fact to add that just might help us to pinpoint the time when the rain might stop. Then, as so often happens, even in such a short period of time, events and distractions intervened and having been intensely interested in the precise timing for a day or so, life went on as usual and so did the rain.

"I didn't know it was possible for time to go by so slowly," grumbled Ham.

Hibernation

Taking the story of the ark literally throws up a number of questions, none greater than how so many animals could have been adequately fed and looked after in a confined space for nearly a year.

One explanation is that they did not all have to be fed. With the enforced inactivity and the temperature inside the ark, it is possible that a large number of the animals might have gone into hibernation and slept for most of the voyage.

In hot habitats some animals survive in a similar way by a process of aestivation, which protects them from heat and conserves their energy, so that they need little or no food or water.

Even humans are known to have practiced a form of semi-hibernation. Well into the 20th century cave dwellers, or troglodytes, in the south of France spent the harsh winters inside sleeping, thus lowering their metabolic rate and enabling them to subsist on a diet of water and dry biscuits, which they consumed intermittently.

eↄᐃↄ

Chapter 14

"When the rain stops, will the sun come out? And if the sun comes out, will all the animals that have been sleeping wake up? And if they wake up will there be enough food to feed them all until the water subsides? And ..."

"That is a lot of questions, daughter," Father said to Arisisah, holding up his hand to quieten her.

Knowing how Father's pronouncements often seemed outrageous to start with but then tended to come true, the rest of us were all ears for at least some of the answers to her questions.

"We will just have to wait and see," was all Father said.

"And I thought he knew everything," muttered Ham.

"What was that, Ham?" said Father whose hearing was still excellent, although he wisely chose to ignore many of the things that he heard.

"I said, you can't be expected to know everything," said Ham going rather red.

"Only God knows everything, Ham," said Father gravely.

"Just what I thought," said Ham looking abashed.

"Do you doubt the word of the Lord?" said Father.

For once Ham had no smart answer or, if he did, he wisely kept it to himself.

So there we were, still trapped inside the ark, with the rain pouring down outside and all of us getting increasingly fractious. The interior that had once seemed so vast to us now seemed stuffy and small. The only part of it where we never ventured was the very front of the ark, where the yetis lived huddled up together, still cowering away from us if anyone disturbed them by going too close.

Then, at last, the rain stopped and we all knew instantly because the constant noise that had been the background to our life all night and all day stopped, just like that.

Immediately, all any of us wanted to do was to get outside as fast as possible. I looked at Salit and beckoned to her to come with me and escape through one of the windows out onto the deck. I was half waiting for Father to call us back, but he did nothing, he just stood there in the gloom with Mother. I was so anxious to unlash the bindings quickly that I fumbled with the fastenings that had tightened up in the wet and it took me twice as long as it should have done. But eventually I managed it, the shutter slammed back and we both scrambled out onto the deck and looked about us.

The strong wind that had been blowing earlier had almost subsided and as we looked over the edge of the ark all we could see was water stretching out flat and dark in every direction, as far as the eye could see. No land, no rocks, nothing protruded from its surface and nothing floated on it, except for the ark. But now that it had stopped raining we could see around us again, even though all we could see was endless water. I put my arm round Salit's shoulders. "I think things may be going to plan after all," I said.

"I do hope you are right," she replied quietly, squeezing my hand.

There was no sun, just grey sky unvaried by clouds stretching away to the horizon. To be honest, even after all this waiting, it wasn't a particularly exciting view. We still had no way of knowing where we were, or where we were going. Somehow, with no way of getting our bearings in this vast grey expanse, I felt almost giddy as I looked around us, as if I might fall down. So I sat down instead and Salit joined me, our backs against the top deck near the window that we had climbed out of. Ham had come out alone and immediately climbed up onto the roof. "I can't see anything," he said, sounding disappointed.

Father and Mother remained inside and on our return Mother

143

appeared more interested than Father to hear about what we had seen.

"In short, Mother, nothing much," said Ham. "Just dark sea and grey sky going on for ever."

"Ah, so have you lost your enthusiasm for the rain stopping already?" asked Father.

"Oh no, that is wonderful," Ham said quickly, almost as if he thought Father had the power to start it again. "We just wondered what's going to happen next."

"We will have to wait and see," said Father enigmatically.

And so we waited and waited all day and nothing else happened. Once the rain had stopped, that was it, no sun, no wind, just the odd wave hardly larger than a ripple across the sea and sometimes far, far away, a rumble, like thunder.

"Oh please God, don't let the rain start again," said Ham.

Meanwhile inside the ark we were able to alleviate the stuffiness at last by letting in some fresh air. We still had to be careful not to let the temperature vary too much or too suddenly, or to create any drafts, which might have caused some of the more sensitive animals to catch a fatal chill. Nor could we risk any of them making a break for freedom.

When Japhet said, "nothing, absolutely nothing, about this experience so far has been easy," I couldn't have agreed more.

After our initial excitement the period after the rain stopped was strangely boring. For what seemed like weeks on end, we had quiet grey days and the unrelieved tedium was almost worse than when it had been raining. I think that we all found ourselves thinking what Ham had already put into words so succinctly, "Now what?"

Needless to say, it was not long before another huge problem arose. With no rain falling to replenish the water in the tanks on the top deck, drinking supplies started to run low and we needed a solution fast. Father looked to Japhet and me to find an answer.

"Well, first let's look at it logically," said Japhet in an authoritative manner.

144

"We're all going to die of thirst?" suggested Ham.

"What would we do on land?" was my tentative contribution.

"Well, we've got plenty of water," said Japhet waving his hand in the direction of the surrounding sea.

"But it is probably salty," said Ham doubtfully.

"Well, there's only one way to find out," I said. "I'll go and fetch a bucket."

"And some rope," Japhet yelled after me, "a lot of rope, it's a long way down."

He was right there, it was a very long way down from the top deck to the water below and I had to knot several pieces of rope together before the bucket could be lowered far enough to reach the water. I drew the bucket back up and Japhet was the first of us to cup his hands and try it for taste. "Not exactly salty," he declared. "There's a bit of a taste of something, but it's quite drinkable."

"Right, good, so it's not too salty or unpleasant to drink, excellent news, but how on earth do we get enough of it from sea level to the roof?" asked Ham.

"In fact, what I'm thinking is, do we need to get it up to the roof level at all? Most of the birds could fly down to reach it at a lower level," said Japhet.

"You're absolutely right," I said. "Thank goodness for that."

"And the water is very calm now," continued Japhet, "so as long as that continues, surely it would be safe to bring the water into the ark at a much lower level?"

"And how are we going to do that?" asked Ham.

"Wait. Just give me time to think," said Japhet. "I need to go away on my own and think about it."

Sure enough Japhet did come up with an answer: the pipes from the tanks on the roof were used to suction water onto the ark by being secured on the bottom deck and siphoned off on the decks above. The end of the pipe that was submerged in the water around the ark was at a higher level than the end of the pipe in the bottom of the ark. Japhet's scheme worked. The problem was solved and the rest of us were hugely impressed.

A Global Flood?

Stories of a great flood are told worldwide and feature in the chronicles of many of the world's great religions. However, geologists dispute that there is any scientific evidence to support this assertion. Perhaps the description in the Bible can be interpreted in the same way as the days of creation, in that it is not meant to be taken literally, according to modern understanding. The people of that era had a far more limited life experience and perhaps it was just a terrible local flood, rather than a worldwide one?

Literalists believe that the rock formations geologists claim were created over millions of years are actually layers of compressed sediment, the result of a worldwide flood that occurred only a few thousand years ago. They argue that if the flood was only a local flood, why did Noah have to build an ark? Why didn't he and his family simply escape from the flooded area to somewhere safe? And if the flood did not cover the whole earth, why did the Old Testament say that all the mountains were submerged? If the flood described in Genesis had been only a local flood, the water would simply have seeped away.

The scriptures describe a flood where the "fountains of the great deep" broke through the earth's crust resulting in earthquakes, volcanoes and geysers spewing molten lava and boiling water. This was said to have continued for 150 days and such conditions would have almost obliterated life on earth; later discoveries of vast numbers of fossilised remains could be evidence of this event.

Once the flood was over, God promised Noah that there would be no more floods of such magnitude again and he created the rainbow as the sign of his covenant. Although there have been many terrible local floods since then, such as the tsunami in Asia in 2004, there has never been another one so severe that it threatened all life on earth.

Chapter 15

❦

T hen gradually, almost imperceptibly, the sky began to lighten. First a narrow band of light formed on the horizon, between the dark of the sea and the blanket grey of the sky. Then we were able to make out the very faint shapes of clouds moving, light against dark above us, and we even imagined that we could see the faintest tinge of blue showing through the grey.

Then the sun returned. On the first day that we saw it, it was partly obscured by clouds, but by the next morning it was fully visible again, too bright for anyone to look at directly. And we realised just how much we had missed seeing it – something that we had always taken for granted before the flood. Its reappearance was even more exciting than the day the rain stopped, and everyone's morale simply soared. The atmosphere of gloom on the ark started to drift away and all of us felt happier.

Now that there was clear sky above us again and we could see the sun in the day and the moon and the stars at night, a kind of normality returned and our days were punctuated by light and dark. At last, things were beginning to get back to how they had been, or as much as they could be in the circumstances, afloat with all the animals in the confined space of the ark, instead of on dry land.

We had deliberately made the windows of the ark small to protect us from the storm and they didn't let in much light. So, in spite of the brightness of the sun outside, it was still rather dark inside the body of the ark and we still had to light candles to see what we were doing. But at least we could leave the shutters open and let the fresh air in and musty animal smells out. Even the smallest shafts of sunlight brightened things up and everything seemed that much fresher. Best of all, we could go outside in the daylight whenever we liked and feel the sun on our skins again.

Unfortunately, in our enthusiasm, some of us forgot the sun's less pleasant effects and it wasn't long before Ham got burnt and Japhet succumbed to sun fever. Father was not impressed: "Look at Shem, he has more common sense than the two of you could put in a ladle," he said irritably. In fact my common sense had nothing to do with it, I just spent more time inside and it was enough for me to know that I could go outside whenever I pleased, without being drenched with rain.

Being able to see the rising and setting of the sun again gave the birds their cue for the start and end of the day, and they began to sing like they used to. We were all in such a good mood, that to start with even the return of the full morning chorus and the raucous cry of the cockerel were welcome. But, needless to say, it wasn't long before we were all complaining again and Ham was looking murderously at the bird.

What is more, fairly soon there were several more cockerels and together they all made so much noise that we had to put covers over them at night, to trick them into keeping quiet for longer, removing them the next morning when it suited us. When we uncovered them they still made a considerable amount of noise, but it didn't last for so long and we could cope with it better when we'd had a little more time to wake up. Ham made quite a ritual of their daily unveiling, whisking the cloth off their cage and taking bets with whoever was about on how long it would be before the first one crowed. It wasn't long before all of us knew that it was as long as it took them to fill their lungs with air, almost exactly on a count of three.

The birds were free to enter and leave the ark at any time, but we didn't think it was wise to completely open the roof. Father was worried that some of the more foolish birds might get caught up in the excitement of a mass exodus and fly away to drown, before they realised the ark was, as yet, the only place on which to perch.

The two magpies were soon causing problems again, initially

having been reluctant to enter the ark. Now they were only too keen to get outside and stay outside, sitting on the ridge of the roof snapping and squawking disagreeably at any of the smaller birds that ventured anywhere near them.

"Those bloody birds!" Ham roared. "I'm sure I saw one of them eat a humming bird earlier."

"Oh, I shouldn't think so," said Japhet. "Much too fast for them for them to catch."

I hoped he was right.

On the domestic front, our wives were now able to hang all the washing outside where it dried far more easily and this seemed to excite them. In fact, the sun was so hot in the heat of the day that if any of us wanted to go outside we realised that we would have to rig up an awning on the deck for shade.

Needless to say we still had all our usual chores to do and the light had woken up some of the sleeping animals, so now we actually had more work. But nothing seemed quite so hard now that we could go out on deck whenever we liked, and watch the sun or the moon glistening on the ripples of the sea. Instead of huddling up on our beds in terror as the ark was buffeted by the huge waves and celestial storms, we were lulled to sleep by the gentle lapping of water against the sides of the ark.

Japhet's ingenious method of providing water to every level of the ark had actually made watering the animals easier for us than before. It involved numerous pipes and estimations of water levels but, thank God, it worked. We still used the smallest of the tanks on the roof, but only to bathe in and to store any excess fish that we caught. The tanks were also very popular with the regular drinking-water swimmers who enthusiastically availed themselves of the open-air facilities. But as a precaution, in case we weren't there to prevent anything from getting trapped and drowning, we put small ramps up the side. Sadly, in spite of this, there were still a few casualties, but never the right ones, as Ham pointed out.

Now that the rain had stopped, replenishing the water in the roof tanks was an onerous task and a never-ending chore as the water quickly evaporated in the heat of the sun. We tried to think of something large enough to cover them during the day but, apart from the woven mats we had which would have shed dust and debris into the water, we had nothing suitable. Every evening when it was cooler, we took it in turns to pull a few buckets of water up from sea level, and it was only the pleasure that everyone had from splashing about in the tanks that made such an effort worthwhile.

After so long on the ark, it had become second nature to all of us to keep an eye on the animals as we went round their stalls and enclosures. It was vitally important to check that they were healthy, not trapped anywhere or inexplicably missing from their stalls or containers, and that they had enough food. The danger of extinction was ever-present and, whenever an animal or bird was lost, the mournful partner who remained was a constant reproach to us.

"What will they do?" Arisisah asked. "Will they just die out?"

"Oh they'll probably cross-breed," said Japhet airily. "There'll be some interesting new mixes, maybe even better than before."

"Well don't let that idea lead to any of you relaxing your vigilance," said Father who had overheard him. "We have been entrusted by God to look after his creatures, not to mess about with them."

"No, Father," we all dutifully answered in unison and even Ham sounded as if he meant it this time.

In spite of the sun and the stars and no longer being terrified by the noise of raging storms, life on the ark was still difficult. Unexpectedly Japhet, who at the beginning was the one that found it the most difficult, now appeared to be coping with life on board the best of us all. This was largely because he had found a very agreeable way to pass his time that was even less strenuous than his old job of looking after the sheep and useful, too, so absolutely perfect for him.

Fishing from the side of the ark every afternoon had become his passion and he soon became very skilled at it. He would sit quietly on edge of the top deck for hours on end, with his lines trailing down into the water, surrounded by cats, otters and sea birds, sitting vigilantly on the rails. All of them intently scanned the surface for any sign of the shoals of fish that usually followed in our wake, attracted by the trail of refuse that constantly floated behind us. We all benefited from this, as it had been decided that whilst it would have seemed tactless to cook meat on board, there didn't seem to be any reason to have such scruples about cooking fish, so things in the food line had definitely improved.

Arisisah was particularly happy about Japhet's new hobby because now she always knew where to find him. They would sit together under the canopy that he had rigged up, talking and fishing, or just sitting in companionable silence, interrupted only by the purring of the ark cats or the otters larking about. It wasn't long before the otters realised they did better if they caught the fish we were storing in the holding tanks rather than sunbathing with the cats and waiting for a share of the catch to come their way. They only caught what they needed to eat, and were so endearing to look at, in spite of their fearsome ability to catch fish, that none of us really minded. And so far there were only two of them.

As usual, it was Ham who found it the hardest to settle down to anything. He tried fishing, but he had so little patience that his restlessness took all the pleasure out of it for Japhet. He had never been an enthusiastic handyman, although he had done more than his share in building the ark. But now that was finished, all this spare time hung heavy on his hands. He moaned constantly that he was bored and he missed the land and his old companions, who were dead. Not only that, the sun was too hot, the ark was too stuffy and there was nothing to talk to the rest of us about that we hadn't already discussed at great length a million times before.

"If I didn't know better, I'd think we had a large spoilt child on board," Japhet observed.

Then, by chance, one of the giraffes ate Nahlat's favourite hair comb, which had been hanging from the wall in our living quarters. Presumably as the comb had swung with the motion of the ark, it had fallen from its peg and slid to where it had caught the giraffe's attention then, with a few crunches, it was gone. Well, Nahlat couldn't have made more fuss if the rain had started again. "What am I going to do? It was a special comb; I'll never get another like it. In fact, I'll never get another comb at all. No, I don't want to borrow one, I want that one back." The giraffe's contented chewing made that an unlikely prospect and watching it swallow and then being able to see the lump of the chewed comb as it travelled slowly down the length of its long neck didn't help. They hadn't annoyed anyone so much since they had finally managed to eat one of Father's vines that they'd had their eyes on ever since they embarked. Father took this badly; in fact he was so furious that if they had been smaller I think they would both have ended up overboard.

As Nahlat's husband, Ham bore the brunt of her rage, so it behove him to think of some way to placate her. She had obtained the lost comb from a travelling peddler years ago; it had special long teeth, which were absolutely perfect for her thick, lustrous, black hair and she'd never get another like it.

"I could make you one," said Ham. "How hard can it be?" So he carved an almost exact replica and, amazingly, Nahlat was delighted with it. After this success he made combs for Salit, Arisi-sah and Mother, all with the personal modifications that they had requested and they were all delighted.

That was the start of Ham's carving phase. From then on he made all sorts of useful things, as well as trinkets for our wives, models of the animals, ornate wooden boxes, everything that could possibly be made from wood. And the more experienced he became, the more beautiful the things he made became. So while Japhet fished, Ham sat carving and modelling, the wood shavings curling around him, quietly basking in everyone's admiration. He even got Mother's spinning wheel working again.

Everything seemed to be going well, as far as I could tell when, for no apparent reason, I became ill. It was quite different from the symptoms of seasickness all of us knew only too well, and could not have been that as the water around the ark was calmer than an oasis pool. It began on a particularly hot day as I made my way inside, out of the heat of the sun and down to the relative gloom of the living quarters. Despite the heat and humidity inside I felt shivery cold and was overcome with such a feeling of nausea that I had to make a quick dash for the soil baisin. 'Please, please let it have been emptied!' I prayed, but no, it was almost full. 'Oh God have mercy on me, I'm not going to make it . . .' and unfortunately, while I was close, I missed the baisin. I felt so ill I couldn't even work out who had missed their turn to do this most unpopular of daily tasks. Then, feeling too bad to do anything about it myself, I staggered to my bed and curled up under the cover, which is where Salit found me later.

I could hardly talk I felt so ill and in spite of numerous helpful suggestions, all I really wanted was to be left alone. Sometimes I felt as cold as a winter's night in the mountains and sometimes I felt as hot as fire. For days I couldn't eat at all and survived on small sips of water. All I wanted to do was to roll up and die; extinction would have been a welcome release from my misery. It didn't occur to me that if I died it would spoil part of God's plan, so it was unlikely to come to that.

I moved out of our living quarters and slept in a comfortable bed Mother had made for me in the straw, as my thrashing about and groaning in the night made it quite impossible for Salit, or indeed anyone else, to get any rest. And none of the remedies that anyone suggested seemed to help at all. None of Arisisah's or Mother's potions would stay down, only a little water, and I grew so thin and so weak I could hardly talk or move. Salit whispered to me that Father prayed constantly for my recovery, and so did she, but all I really wanted was for everyone to leave me alone.

In the weeks that followed there were many times when the prospect of death seemed infinitely preferable to living, but when I felt Salit's tears of anxiety and fear as she tended to me I knew that I could not give up. What would she do if I died? I had married her, taken her away from her family and made her a member of mine. And, more importantly, I had promised her family that I would look after her. Now I was all she had left in the world. I had to get well, I was her husband and I couldn't leave her on her own.

Very slowly I began to improve and feel better and I couldn't help noticing that the better I felt the less attention everyone seemed to pay to me. And, selfishly, I felt a little put out by this. Admittedly, Salit was still a dutiful wife, but even she did not spend a great deal of time with me anymore. Not that I was without company, though, my bed was alive with cats and dogs sprawled across my feet and as I began to feel better the rats and mice amused me with acrobatic tricks in the straw stacked above me, which often ended with them falling like pebbles onto the bed. Other things rustled in the straw around me too, but I tried not to imagine what they might be.

I also noticed that no one came and asked me how to do things anymore and no one asked my opinion. I realised with painful clarity that I was not nearly as indispensable as I had previously thought that I was. I could have died and life on the ark would have gone on without me. I struggled to find this a comforting thought.

Father came to see how I was one morning. "You must be feeling a little neglected, Shem," he said, sitting carefully on the edge of my bed between two cats, so as not to disturb me too much. "We are all so busy I'm afraid it must seem as if we have forgotten you." He took my hand comfortingly and as I looked up at his kind face and concerned expression, I felt tears of shame prick my eyes.

"No, Father, I realise now that I am not indispensable. God has chosen to save us all for a reason and I realise that we are all equally precious to him."

"Well maybe you are right, Shem," was all he said and, patting me gently on the shoulder, he left me to ponder my new-found insight, uncomfortable as that was.

How quick I had been to notice Japhet's laziness and Ham's impatience and I wondered what they thought about me. I could think of a few possibilities and they did not make for pleasant contemplation. And poor Salit, how much time did I spend with her? I was always busy and there were always more pressing things to do.

Later that day when Salit came to see how I was, she was amazed at how much I had improved. "Nothing short of a miracle," was how she put it, "you look so much better." She was even more surprised when I told her how sorry I was for being an inconsiderate and neglectful husband, who put everything and everyone else before her and how I was going to change. "Not too much, Shem," she said smiling.

The Disappearance of the Floodwaters

From the information given in the book of Genesis, the floodwaters reached their maximum depth after 40 days and nights of continual heavy rain. The waters began to decrease on the 150th day and on the first day of the tenth month the tops of the mountains were visible again. Forty days later, Noah sent out a raven in search of land; it was not successful.

In the next three weeks Noah sent out a dove. The first time it returned, the second time it brought back an olive leaf and the third time the dove did not return at all.

It was over a year before Noah left the ark, on the 371st day after the rains began.

It has been estimated that the waters receded at a rate of about 15 feet a day and with nothing visible to measure this fall against, it would have been impossible for Noah or his family to make a reliable estimation of the water's rate of subsidence.

Chapter 16

❖

A lmost as soon as we first opened the hatches and windows of the ark and went out in the sunlight again, we found new ways to entertain ourselves. Cooped up in the gloom of the ark we had become bored and lethargic.

Now things began to change. We had more energy and needed some kind of entertainment to keep ourselves occupied. We started with throwing contests judged on either distance or accuracy with some sort of imaginary target but, unfortunately, it wasn't long before we were running low on things to throw overboard. There were so few unnecessary items on the ark that there were never very many objects to spare. At first, we used odd sticks and twigs, pebbles we took from the lizards' pen; we tried fruit stones, but date stones were far too small to be much use, and it wasn't long before our armoury was exhausted.

"I can't believe there isn't anything else to throw, there must be something, this is ridiculous," Ham grumbled.

"Well what?" asked Japhet. "If we go on taking things out of the animals' cages they will all be on bare boards soon."

"There must be something," repeated Ham. "No, wait a minute, I've got it, it's ideal, something that no one will mind about, nobody will miss and it won't do anybody any harm; something in fact, that we already throw overboard. Why on earth didn't we think of it before?"

Somehow I didn't like the sound of this, but Japhet was ahead of me. "Not dung?" he asked suspiciously.

"Well, why not?" demanded Ham. "We have to deal with it every day as it is."

"But won't it fall apart?" I asked.

"Not if we dry it," said Ham triumphantly. "Then it will be as hard as stones."

"But won't it be a bit light for throwing?" Japhet queried.

"Not if we roll it up really tight. That will make it dense and heavy enough to throw," answered Ham triumphantly. "We might even dampen them down a bit just before we use them, which would make them heavier."

"Yes, you're right," said Japhet nodding thoughtfully and managing to look both impressed and doubtful at the same time.

My contribution was to suggest that we only use the droppings of herbivores, which the others rapidly agreed to.

So, we added the tight rolling and drying of droppings to our other tasks and Ham was right, they made useable missiles and we could also monitor the size being thrown by each contestant, which made things fairer. Japhet was the most accurate thrower; Ham could throw the furthest; I wasn't much good at either. But both of them had lots of practice under their belts from tending the family flock and having to drive off predators with a hail of well-aimed pebbles when necessary.

From then on we passed many happy evenings in this simple pursuit, with the three of us skimming and throwing the balls of dung as far as we could from the side of the ark, while the women sat quietly talking. It no longer seemed fair to say gossiping, because surely by then there couldn't have been much left for them to gossip about.

"Don't you believe it," said Japhet sagely. "Women would find something to say if you left two of them in the middle of a desert under a palm tree for a year."

"I agree with you there," said Ham. "In fact I am absolutely certain that Nahlat would have plenty to say, if I was foolish enough to do that to her. I think you'll find that most women would."

Now that the sun beat down on the ark all day and there was no shade outside except for Japhet's fishing awning, the temperature inside rose as well. It was uncomfortably hot during the day, although it did get more bearable in the evening. To cool off at the end of the day, first our wives and then we men would splash about in the water tanks. And although I think she secretly enjoyed it as much as the rest of us, Nahlat made a terrible fuss every time because she was frightened of the fish that we kept in the tanks.

Then if we had the energy some of us would lead a few of the smaller and more co-operative animals out onto the deck in turns so that they could cool down in the night air. We tethered them beside us and they stood or lay down quietly, quite unperturbed by our activities. Every evening we laid out cushions for the flute players, usually Japhet and Father, while the rest of us either sat or dozed on rugs strewn around them, listening to them play or quietly chatting while we looked up at the stars or at the moon-light on the sea.

If we were lucky Father would bring out a jug of wine for us to share, otherwise we would have beer. It was the best part of our day, with the moon highlighting a silver path across the sea, stretching away from the ark towards the dark line of the far horizon. The only other movements were the swooping and gliding of the birds and bats rising on the warm air currents around the ark at dusk and the soft shuffling of the animals tethered beside us, quietly enjoying the cool of the night air.

Sometimes someone, usually Ham, would break the silence by saying something like "Which is your favourite animal or bird?" or "What are you most looking forward to when – or should that be if – we land?" And one day without thinking, he asked, "Who or what do you miss the most?" and we all ended up in tears.

"My favourite animal is the one that causes me the least trouble," said Japhet suddenly, doing his best to change the subject. "And that means it doesn't eat too much, therefore doesn't make much mess, has a pleasant temperament, doesn't bite or kick and isn't nervous. In fact in an ideal world it might even be hiber-nating."

"You can't choose one that is asleep," said Salit, "that doesn't count."

"So could it be the zebras, then?" enquired Ham innocently.

"No it could not," answered Japhet with some vehemence.

"I'd choose something that is entertaining or interesting in some way," I said, "like the chameleons, or the mynah birds who are the best talkers."

"One of the grey parrots is pretty damn good, though," said Ham, a turn of phrase which earned him one of Father's disapproving looks.

"Well, I wouldn't mind that grey parrot if you had taught it something other than 'There's land!' and 'Is that the rain again?' It shocks me every time," said Mother, trying hard to divert Father's attention. "But the other grey parrot doesn't speak at all I've noticed. Why do you think that is?"

"It's probably the male and can't get a word in edgeways," said Ham.

"I suppose the dog is my favourite animal really," said Japhet seriously. "He keeps me company."

"What about a creature that is useful?" I said. "Give me a good donkey or a camel or even a sheep any day."

"But none of them are useful now," Japhet said, "so what's the point of choosing them?"

"Well you could ask what the point of your dog, is then," I retorted. "It wouldn't be any use as a sheep dog, even on dry land, so where's the usefulness in that?"

Japhet looked rather hurt at these words. "I never said that I liked him because he is useful, I like him because he keeps me company, like my shadow. He just follows me about because he wants to, it's as if he chose me, it's just in his nature."

Now, because I had offended him, it was my turn to change the subject and make amends by asking everyone the first thing that came into my head which was: "What, if any, do you think the benefits of being on the ark are?"

"Oh, where shall I start?" said Japhet at once. "Cooped up with my whole family in a very small space, with more animals to look after than I knew existed in my wildest imaginings, eating almost the same food every day and knowing all our old friends and neighbours are drowned. Not knowing where we are, not having a home any more, having nothing to look at but sky and sea. I could go on," he added, quickly reeling off an impressive list of grievances.

"Are you sure you haven't missed something?" I asked with just a touch of sarcasm. Perhaps it hadn't been the best choice of question.

"Japhet, Shem, enough!" said Father sharply, raising his hand for silence.

Ham

Ham is thought to have been Noah's youngest son, but he is also referred to as his middle son. He was the Father of Canaan, who was cursed by Noah.

After the flood, the family settled down together and Noah farmed the land and cultivated his vines for wine. One day Ham found his Father naked and drunk in his tent. Instead of just leaving him to sober up, or covering him up, he thought it would be amusing to bring his brothers to the tent to see the state Noah was in. But, having respect for their Father, they did not look at him and averted their eyes while they covered him over. When Noah found out what had happened, he flew into a rage and cursed Ham's son Canaan, saying he and his descendants would be the servants of his brothers.

Noah cursed Canaan not Ham, with whom he was furious, because the wellbeing of one's children was regarded as of more importance than that of oneself and would therefore hurt Ham more.

Ham's descendants settled in North Africa, Libya, Egypt, Ethiopia and the region also known as Canaan. It has been said that Ham was the founder of all the black races and being a descendant of the cursed Canaan has even been put forward as a justification for slavery.

 e⌒∧⌒e

Chapter 17

⊰◈⊱

There were many ways in which our life on the ark was difficult. Things constantly went wrong and plans went awry; the animals could be awkward and temperamental and the longer we were all confined together, the more we got on each other's nerves and the more frequently we had disagreements. Although we knew that at heart he was really the kindest of men, we were all a bit afraid of Father. This sometimes led us to hiding our mistakes, or trying to avoid responsibility for things that had gone wrong, which usually meant that things got even worse. And he always found out what had happened anyway.

Every day I watched Japhet rush through his inside chores in a more and more slapdash manner and anything he thought that he could get away with not doing he didn't do at all. Of course he fed and watered all his animals – he would never have neglected to do that – but he became very lazy about mucking out their stalls and they always looked dirtier than the stalls that Ham and I were responsible for. And every day he managed to be up on deck fishing before Ham and I were even half way through our work although, to be fair, I must admit that by now we weren't always that diligent ourselves.

As for Ham, his jokes and outspokenness, which I used to find such a welcome respite from the seriousness of our situation, had begun to grate on my nerves. And of course when he realised that he was irritating me, I swear he got even worse. But in spite of his incessantly chirpy mood and breathtakingly tactless outbursts he still made me laugh and he did have some good ideas. He had noticed Japhet's increasingly lazy ways as well and we decided that it was time to teach him a lesson.

One day we both got up extra early, long before Japhet normally stirred. After fishing the morning swimmers out of the drinking troughs – a platypus and two otters I think it was that day – we crept down to the lower stalls and set to work collecting as much dung as we could from all the animals in the stalls around the zebras, which we then threw over the partition into the zebras' pen. As I've mentioned before, the zebras were disagreeable animals at the best of times and having their stall half-filled with the droppings of other animals did nothing to improve their mood. A lot of stamping and snorting went on, while Ham and I stifled our giggles like two shepherd boys. Once we had gone as far as we could, without actually throwing droppings all over the zebras, we retreated and continued with our normal everyday duties, while we waited with some anticipation for Japhet to appear.

As luck would have it, that morning Japhet was even later than usual, and by the time he arrived on the lower deck, Ham and I were working in stalls some distance away from the zebras. We heard him humming loudly to himself as he fed and watered the first of his animals, so we knew he was getting closer and closer to the zebras' stall and we were all ears. Then at last we heard the most terrible roar: "Tiger's testicles and bat's blood, what did you two eat last night?" At this, the two zebras jumped forward in their pen, alarmed at his outburst and already unhappy with the cramped and unpleasant conditions they were now in.

"Some of Arisisah's herb stew, I expect," said Ham under his breath, "it has that effect on me." With that I almost choked laughing and Ham, who was well-pleased with himself by now, started laughing as well.

With such an abnormally large amount of droppings in the zebra stall, Japhet couldn't simply throw them over the partition into the passage, as he would normally have done; he had to open the gate and pull the droppings sack to the entrance. But, on seeing the open gate, the zebras who were bored and also irritated by the invasion of their stall barged their way out into the passageway,

164

thundering through the huge pile of droppings, splattering it all the way up the passage. By now Japhet was absolutely beside himself with rage and Ham and I watched helpless with mirth as the zebras cantered up the passageway, slipping and sliding on the remnants of dung they had scattered from their stall. The ensuing uproar caught the attention of Nahlat, who shouted down to us to ask what was going on.

"Don't come down here," warned Ham. "The zebras have escaped from their stall, and you know what they can be like."

"But how did they escape?" Nahlat shouted back, amidst the uproar.

"They, they, oh ..." here Ham had trouble in continuing... "They had stomach trouble last night ... stall full of dung, you can imagine, and whilst Japhet was clearing it up they escaped." And as he spoke the zebras, who by now had gathered a considerable amount of speed, shot past us for the second time, with a puce-faced Japhet in hot pursuit but still some way behind them.

By now, the noise and shouting had attracted the attention of Salit and Arisisah, who had come down to the middle deck to see what the rumpus was about. They looked down, bemused, as they watched the pandemonium that had broken out.

"Shall I go and fetch Father?" asked Arisisah.

"Oh heavens no, definitely not! I don't think there's very much he could do, thanks," I shouted up to her. "Don't worry, we can sort it out."

"I think we'll just have to wait until those two have run out of puff," Ham added.

"I can't think what happened," croaked Japhet as he collapsed on some straw beside us. "Did you ever see so much dung? It made the elephants look positively constipated."

The uneven race between Japhet and the zebras finally ended with Ham coming to his rescue and cornering them at the very front of the ark. They had disturbed the two yetis, which was unfortunate, and they both rose up out of their bedding looking startled and dishevelled, rubbing their eyes in the light. The zebras were equally taken aback by the yetis, who towered over the rebellious pair as they finally slid to a halt.

"Sorry," Ham said to the yetis. "I think we've got them now," and with that he slipped a rope round the neck of one of the zebras and, with the other meekly following, he led them both back to their stall.

By now Japhet had cleared out the rest of the droppings from their stall and the two stripy animals, their flanks heaving with exertion from this unaccustomed exercise, settled down and started to pull at the net of hay that he had hung up for them, as if nothing had happened.

"Hey Japhet, you don't think those two ought to fast for a day or so after all that?" asked Ham helpfully.

"Only if it's you that goes in there now and tries to take their food away," responded Japhet.

Later on, when we had all gathered together for our midday meal and Father asked us how the morning had gone; it seemed prudent not to mention Japhet's problems with the zebras. He still did not seem to have realised that Ham and I were involved, but we didn't want to push our luck with Father, who might have smelled a rat. And fortunately for us Japhet had no reason to dwell on a story that put him in a poor light, so nothing more was said.

Shem

_____

Shem was Noah's oldest son; his name means 'name', 'fame', or possibly 'dusky'. He was the forefather of the Semitic peoples who were named after him and used similar language and culture. Amongst them were the Israelites/Hebrews through his descendant Eber, and he was the forefather of both Abraham, the Father of Israel, and of Jesus. The Semite people were descendants of Shem alone, not of his brothers Ham and Japhet.

Shem's eldest son Elam was the head of a clan of Israelites who settled in Jerusalem after God dispersed the inhabitants of Babylon, where the sons of Noah had initially congregated after leaving Noah. Their descendants built a great city of brick and tar and a tower (the Tower of Babel) that reached towards the heavens. This was contrary to God's wishes so finally, instead of there being one common language understood by everyone, God confused this language into many, so the people could no longer understand each other; this forced them to disperse and they left Babylon.

Shem's descendants settled mainly in the region of Mesopotamia and also ruled in Syria, Palestine, Chaldea and Arabia. The Canaanites, who were the descendants of Ham, settled in these regions as well.

☙❧

Chapter 18

✦

After so long on the ark our daily routine hardly varied and all of us knew exactly what had to be done and how to do it. I certainly could have done all my chores in my sleep. More and more of the animals had become subdued by the warmth inside the ark and even more of them just slept or dozed most of the time. Even the ones that did stay awake no longer seemed particularly keen to go outside in the fresh air, so in the end we didn't bother to take them; Japhet's indolence must have been catching. So as time went by we had less and less to do and our initial excitement at seeing the sun and going outside had waned. Very little happened, the days dragged and life on the ark was extremely monotonous.

By now we had all been confined together for so long that there was nothing we hadn't discussed, no story untold, no memory unexplored and no hopes for the future that we had not already shared with each other. We were so overcome with lethargy and boredom that we no longer wondered what would happen to us or when it would happen, or even really cared about much anymore. During our endless family discussions we had speculated about every possibility from the mundane to the fantastical and as we had no way of determining our future all we could do was wait.

Unfortunately, by now we had lost count of the days that had passed after the 40 days and 40 nights' excitement because at some stage Mother and Arisisah had both been marking them off on the wall, so now the whole thing was in a hopeless mess. No one said much when we found out, as it wouldn't have made things any better and would only have upset them both even more. But it was a real blow and made us feel even more out of control; Ham actually cried when he found out.

Only two really notable things had happened since our embarkation: the rain had stopped and the sun had reappeared. By now, at a very rough estimate, we had spent seven or eight months floating about with absolutely nothing new or interesting to look at, just endless water stretching to the horizon. No wonder it didn't take very much to cause an upset, and losing track of time certainly did that. As usual, all Father said was that we must "leave it up to God" or something to that effect, but by now even that didn't irritate us as much as it used to.

Our wives were far better at occupying themselves with their daily tasks than we men were. None of them seemed particularly bothered by what was, or rather wasn't, happening. Nor did they seem particularly interested in speculating how long our current situation was going to last, even less so now that their counting system had imploded.

As for the men, I think we were more used to keeping things to ourselves, although we still occasionally discussed some of the possible alternatives for our future: supposing the water never went; if and when it did, where would it all go; supposing it drained away over the edge of the world and all of us went with it, and so on. Father had assured us that the water would go without being at all specific as to how, so we were still in the dark. Thinking logically, we knew that there were a number of ways the water could disappear. It could evaporate, sink in, seep away or simply dry up, but it was an exceptionally large amount of water and we couldn't help wondering if the normal rules, whatever they were, would still apply.

Then, one boiling hot afternoon while I was under Japhet's awning dozing amongst the cushions while he fished, he suddenly shouted out. He thought he saw a splash not that far away from the ark.

"Shem, wake up," he said, shaking me. "I think there's a big one out there, look." Sure enough, I could see an unmistakeable splash as well.

"I think you're right," I said. "Can you feel anything on the line?"

"No, it's too far away at the moment, but I'll cast out again, as far as I can towards it and see what happens."

"That was a big splash; you want to watch out you don't catch something so big that you can't cope with it," I advised.

"Oh it'll be fine," Japhet replied confidently. "Most of the big fish are easy to see or, like the dolphins, they jump right out of the water, so they're hard to miss." And with that he cast his line out again as far as he could in the direction of the turbulence. But although the hook and weight seemed to have landed quite close to where we had seen the splash, nothing took the bait.

"Well, he's a bold fellow," said Japhet. "Most fish would have swum for it by now; it must know something's up."

"I don't think it does," I said.

"Why's that?" Japhet retorted sharply.

"Well I may not know much about fishing," I said, "but I do recognise a rock when I see one."

"A rock?" shouted Japhet, peering into the distance, "It's a rock, you're right!"

"Quick, let's fetch the others," I said. And flinging his rod on the deck with a clatter, Japhet followed me into the ark, both of us yelling, "LAND, LAND!" at the tops of our voices.

It wasn't long before our shouting had roused everyone from their afternoon rest and into a state of near hysteria. Following our excited directions they all lined up at the railings on the east side of the ark, anxiously looking at the waves created by the rock emerging from the water. The only thing that tempered our excitement was Salit's reminder that this was virtually identical to the last thing we had seen before the floodwaters finally covered over all the land. When she said this, Nahlat and Arisisah, who were both overwrought with emotion and excitement, burst into tears and had to be gently comforted by Mother. Even Father rubbed his eyes with his sleeve, although he turned away from the rest of us to do so. But when I looked round to see Ham's reaction he wasn't there, which wasn't like him at all; he never liked to miss anything.

Once Nahlat realised that Ham must still be asleep, she pulled away from Mother and ran back inside the ark to wake him. Shortly afterwards they emerged, Ham looking half awake and blinking in the strong sunlight.

"Nahlat said something about land?" he mumbled hesitantly, still half asleep. But when we directed his attention to the unmistakeable point of a rock sticking out of the water, he soon woke up.

"LAND!" he shrieked, even more loudly than Japhet and I had just done and then, looking at it again, more calmly this time, he said, "It's a rock. Well, it's a start."

Some of us laughed and some of us cried and I saw that Father had wandered up to the front of the ark and was down on his knees in prayer.

Over the next few days we floated around the rock and more and more of it rose above the surface of the water and then another rock appeared close by. By now we were so excited that even when Japhet pointed out that the summit of a mountain range would not be at all suitable to land on, it didn't dampen our spirits.

Only a few months ago it would have seemed unthinkable that we would get so much comfort from the sight of two rocks but now, after all we had been through, we did. The rocks were the first things I wanted to see when I got up in the morning and the last thing I checked on before I went to my bed at night. They were the first definite sign that something was happening at last. Or so we all thought.

And then they disappeared.

The ark, a vessel without sails, that we had no way of steering, had simply drifted away from the two peaks in the night. And although in our hearts we knew that Japhet had been right, and that landing on the summit of a mountain, surrounded by fathoms of water, would have been a disaster, we still couldn't help feeling painfully disappointed.

"Nothing but bloody water again," said Ham, speaking for all of us.

It was difficult to decide whether having seen the mountain summits and then lost sight of them again was worse than not having seen them at all. And we had plenty of time to discuss these options at length. But, in the ensuing weeks, when we saw no more rocks or any signs of land whatsoever, it almost seemed as if we might have imagined it all. Or perhaps we had simply had a vision. Had the rocks been a mirage that we thought we had seen rising out of the water? Or a figment of our imaginations, just something that we thought we had seen because we were all so anxious to see land?

"Don't worry," said Japhet philosophically. "Something else will happen soon."

But nothing did.

The days continued to go by as uneventfully as before and all we could see was water. Then it was weeks and still no more land, no mirages of land, nothing but water. Then it must have been about a month, maybe two months, and still nothing changed. But seeing the mountaintops had unsettled us; we had been so elated when we saw them and so upset when they disappeared that now all of us desperately wanted to see more land. As usual, Father prayed for guidance, but if he was given any he didn't share it.

"What we need is a lookout," suggested Japhet. "The giraffes would be ideal, wouldn't they?"

"Well apart from the fact that the giraffes are quite timid and I'm not quite sure how on earth we could get them out on the top deck, it is a great idea," I said diplomatically.

"I didn't know that they could speak either," added Ham sarcastically.

"What about one of the birds?" suggested Arisisah.

"One of the talking birds," said Nahlat.

"The parrots and the mynah birds can already say 'There's land' and 'Is that the rain again?'" said Mother, "such useful phrases, in the circumstances. You taught them that didn't you, Ham?" she said with just a touch of sarcasm in her voice, which was very unlike her.

172

"Well no, we wouldn't know if they were just saying it and, what's more, they can't fly very far either," said Ham, unabashed.

So while a bird was definitely a good idea, it was important to choose one that was suitable for the task. What we really needed was a good strong flyer. The water birds already flew around the ark every day diving for fish and the gulls followed in the wake of the ark scavenging for food. But none of the other birds flew about very much, probably because they didn't want to risk being left behind.

"What about one of the albatrosses?" said Japhet. "I've heard that they sometimes fly so far, that if they need to they can actually fly in their sleep."

"Well that's no good then. We might lose it and if it can fly for such a long time without landing we might have to wait days for it to return. Then, of course, when it did come back, if it came back, how would we know whether it had landed or not?" said Ham.

"True," said Japhet slowly digesting what Ham had just said, before continuing. "What we need is a strong flyer with intelligence, a bird that needs to land within a reasonable time and wants to return to the ark even if it does find land. So then we would know that if it had been gone for longer than it can fly without resting, it must have landed somewhere before coming back to us."

"Exactly," agreed Father. "Just give me some time to think this through; it's important to make the right choice." There was a long silence before he said "What about a raven?"

"Just the thing," said Japhet nodding his approval. "They're strong and intelligent, very loyal to their mate, so they'd want to come back and they need to land within a fairly short space of time."

"Yes, ideal Father, good choice," enthused Ham. "Except how will we get the male to leave his mate in the first place? And of course we'll have to be careful she doesn't go too, we need her to stay behind as bait to lure him back and make sure he returns if he

173

does find land. Have you noticed what a devoted couple they are?"

Father nodded a little bleakly.

"Ravens aren't stupid, far from it," said Ham. "They like to land in trees or rocks and it will be blindingly obvious to it when it gets up on the roof of the ark that there are neither in the vicinity. I don't know how we are going to encourage it to leave the ark and fly about.

Father settled it. "All we can do is to try and get the raven to fly away from the ark and then see what happens. I really think it is about time we tried something and somehow I feel that God would approve of this, so let's give it a go."

"Have you had any special instructions then, Father?" asked Ham innocently.

"No," said Father. "But I am sure that God will be with us."

The first difficulty we had to overcome was trying to entice one of the ravens out of the bird loft and away from its mate. And, as any disturbance amongst the birds always resulted in a blizzard of droppings, none of us was particularly keen to volunteer.

"Just put a piece of fish on a long pole and wave it about in front of the ravens," said Arisisah, who was obviously more desperate for something to happen than I had realised. That didn't actually work, because the pole wasn't long enough to reach the middle of the perch where the two ravens were ensconced; instead it was snapped up by one of the seagulls that were always ravenous and very quick off the mark where food was concerned. Then we dangled a piece of fish on a short length of rope through one of the roof openings directly above them. The male was definitely interested and seized the fish hungrily, but it still didn't budge. It gulped the fish down greedily and the only reaction we got was one of rage from the female raven, clearly extremely put out at not getting fed as well.

"Maybe now she'll nag him so much that he'll want to leave," suggested Japhet, looking sideways at Arisisah.

"Well I don't think we can really rely on that," I said. "Oh look out, the female's so jealous about the food that she's flying up after the rope the fish was lowered down on... There you go, she's come out."

"Quick, quick, shut the roof or the male will follow her!" cried Salit anxiously.

So now we had the female raven on the roof and the male left inside on the perch, croaking fire and brimstone at the loss of his mate. This was not quite how we had planned it, but we couldn't see any particular reason why the female raven couldn't do the job just as well. We still had the problem of trying to get the huge bird to leave the ark and take off from its perch on the roof, though. Arisisah ran to get a broom from inside and on her return she rushed towards the raven brandishing it about and making shooing sounds. The raven that had just been looking around at the view was startled into flight, spreading her wings to show us her impressive wing span, before taking off, only to land almost immediately just a little further up the roof from her tormentor.

"Oh, what are we going to do now? She's just not budging," groaned Ham.

"Try throwing some fish into the water and see if she follows it – that might get her airborne again at the very least," said Father.

"Good idea," said Japhet, throwing some of his morning catch high into the air to catch the raven's attention.

To everyone's relief, this seemed to work. The raven took off, greedy for her share of the fish pieces and, having caught one, gulped it down and started circling and swooping round the ark like an acrobat, until even though the ark was only moving on slowly she got slightly left behind.

"Look at her go!" shouted Ham.

"Except she's not exactly going, is she?" I said. "She's just circling round the ark playing games."

"We need her to go much further away. It has to be further than we can already see ourselves for it to be any use at all," said Father with a sigh. And of course he was right. We tried in vain to get the raven to fly off, but nothing we could think of would get her to leave us. Whether it was the sound of her mate's outraged prot-estations from inside the ark keeping her back, or that she simply sensed that there was nothing else of interest away from the ark, she just wouldn't leave. Finally, after half an hour or so of looping the loop and flying high above the ark, she landed gracefully back on the roof and nothing we could do would make her take off again. She simply sidled away from us out of reach. In the end there was nothing for it but to allow her back to her mate, who had never ceased cawing and croaking loudly for her return, while he hopped and jumped up and down with agitation on their section of the perching pole inside the roof.

Although the outcome had been disappointing, this was a great deal more excitement than we were used to and by the end of the day we were all so exhausted that we retired to our beds earlier than usual.

Next morning nothing had changed and life went on as usual, with feeding, mucking out the stalls and all our familiar grumbles and gripes. No land was visible from the deck of the ark but Japhet promised to keep an eye out while he fished, which cunningly made him sound twice as busy as he really was.

By the middle of the day when we had a small meal together before resting, it seemed to me that yesterday had just been forgotten. I started to question how much longer things would go on like this ... Would I, or rather we, be able to go on coping with the situation if nothing else happened soon?

Japhet

Documentation is unclear as to whether Japhet was the eldest, middle or youngest son of Noah. After the dispersal from Sumer where Noah's sons first settled after leaving him, Japhet's descendants spread far and wide, populating the northern countries of Europe, from France to Asia Minor (Turkey) and as far afield as India and Russia.

The original Sumerian settlement eventually evolved into the infamous city of Babel, part of the first major civilisation in Mesopotamia and, indeed, the world. Settling down there together was in direct contravention of God's command to Noah and his sons that they should "spread out over the face of the earth". Not only that but, under the command of King Nebuchadnezzar, the people of Babel started to build a vast temple (The Tower of Babel), a great seven-stepped pyramid called a ziggurat, topped by a temple to Marduk, the god of Babylon, rather than to the glory of Noah's one God. It is thought that ziggurats were built as artificial mountains to reach up towards the gods not, as is sometimes stated, to reach heaven.

God's confusion of the common language of Babylonians led to the building of the temple being ceased, as people began to migrate and populate other areas, thus finally fulfilling his original wishes.

☙❧

Chapter 19

⬥

Only too soon the excitement that we had felt at seeing the rocks appear in the sea and their subsequent disappearance followed by our lack of success with the raven, dissipated any optimism we might have felt and we were once again mired in disappointment and apathy. By now we were becoming very used to disappointment, so we were surprised when Father spoke to us again less than a week later and said he felt we should have another go at sending out a bird and that this time we should try a dove. I wondered if it wouldn't be too much to hope that Father might have taken a little advice from above; he seemed so sure of his choice this time and he hadn't asked for our suggestions. But not even Ham dared to ask him outright if this was actually the case, so we couldn't be sure.

"Doves are not as smart as ravens," Japhet said with authority. "Ravens are some of the smartest birds there are."

I'm not sure how this was meant to be encouraging. Maybe the raven's lack of enthusiasm for flying away into the far distance, with no sign of anything to land on, was indeed an indication of its smartness? I couldn't say.

Fortunately everything went much more smoothly with the doves and, smart or not, they were far easier to deal with than the ravens had been. For a start, we found them both perching peacefully at the end of a roof pole and they were placid and tame by nature, so when Father asked Japhet to fetch one down it was a far easier task. Once he had hold of it, we all trooped up on deck to watch its ceremonial release. This time there was no flying straight back to the ark and, as if guided by a divine hand, or so we all hoped, the dove flew off in a northwesterly direction so swiftly that it wasn't long before we could no longer see it.

"Well there you are," said Father with satisfaction. "A much more amenable bird, just what we need."

Once the dove had vanished into the distance, we realised that just standing there looking after it was a waste of time, especially when we all had work to do, so we went back down to the animal decks except Salit who Father chose to stay up on deck as lookout.

"Maybe doves aren't sensible birds at all, just really stupid ones," Ham said suddenly once Father was out of earshot and we were busy feeding the larger animals. "Did you see it go? What on earth did it think it was doing?"

"Oh, I don't know," I said, "but couldn't you just try to remain optimistic for once?" His words had rattled me and then I was impatient with my animals who were all anxious to be fed.

Disappointingly, in spite of all our hopes of divine guidance, the dove returned quite quickly and although Father examined it carefully for any indication that it might have landed somewhere, he found nothing.

"I really do get the feeling that he knows something about those doves that we don't," Salit whispered to me. I wasn't so sure, but I did feel that perhaps it would have been wiser not to send the next one out quite so soon after the last. At this, Salit accused me of being wise after the event and I was tempted to answer her equally sharply. We were all rather on edge.

Then, as so often happens when one thing goes wrong, it turns into one of those days when nothing goes right. Shortly after having words with Salit, I was bitten by a large rat that I had disturbed while it was feeding in one of the grain sacks. My hand bled profusely. It really hurt and I felt like using all the curses I knew.

Then one of the water pipes started to leak at an almost inaccessible point, where it was going to be particularly difficult to deal with, and then it was Japhet's turn to throw a tantrum. Later on Nahlat found moths had made a home in her favourite shawl and

179

when Mother tried to console her, gave her a very ungracious reply. Then Mother, irritated by Nahlat's rudeness, was a little sharp with Arisisah over something trivial and Arisisah ran away to hide at the front of the ark. She had forgotten that was where the yetis lived and her sudden appearance disturbed them so much that shrieking and grunting ensued all round. The commotion distracted Father from his prayers and there were some fairly frank exchanges and recriminations all round.

"Now I suppose it will be ages before we can try another reconnaissance flight," sighed Japhet gloomily, when everything had died down again.

"Well, there are only two doves and they both look pretty much the same so, if Father insists on it being a dove again and he can't tell the difference between them, I don't suppose he will want to tire either of them out by flying them before they have had time to recover," I replied, struggling to keep the glumness out of my voice.

But, exactly a week later, which was pretty quick in ark time, Father stood on the deck again, carefully cradling a dove in his cupped hands. Then, having gently smoothed its feathers, he raised his hands to the sky and the little bird steadied itself on the edge of his palm, before flying up into the air and away. We had all gathered on the deck for this event, more out of politeness this time than with the expectation of anything much happening. And once the dove had disappeared from sight, we immediately went below rather than waste any time waiting for its return, although I think we all expected this to be imminent. But this time the bird took so long to come back that we were all concerned for its safety.

"Maybe it's died of exhaustion," said Japhet, "and just dropped into the sea."

"Thank you for that suggestion, Japhet," said Father, sounding extremely irritated.

"Another extinction then," added Ham, who often missed the cue to keep quiet.

Father had just closed his eyes in exasperation when a loud exclamation from Salit, who had gone back up on the deck, had us all rushing out to join her, clamouring for news of what she had seen.

Excitedly she pointed towards the horizon. And there, coming closer and closer was a tiny dark shape that slowly evolved from a dot into a bird with its wings flapping. As it came closer we could see for certain that it was the white dove returning. It flew, straight as an arrow towards us, until it finally spread out its wings and landed gently on the roof of the ark.

"It's back and it's safe," said Father, "and what's more, this time I think it has got something in its beak."

"Whatever it is, it's very small," said Ham.

"It's a very small bird," said Japhet. "It was never going to fly back with anything large, even a twig would probably have been far too tiring for it to carry for any distance."

While they were bickering, Father had gently enticed the bird down and taken the object from its beak. "It's an olive leaf," he said, gazing at it in wonder then holding the tiny green leaf up for us all to see. "Olive trees don't grow on the peaks of mountains so I think it's safe to say that we have a sign that land is emerging from the sea."

At last, I thought, maybe things are really going to turn out all right and the end is in sight. After all this time I could hardly breathe and tears came to my eyes. I hugged Salit very close to me and silently prayed that I was right.

We should have realised that nothing ever moved swiftly in the great plan of things as far as the ark was concerned. The water was not suddenly going to subside. We were not going to wake up one morning and find ourselves back on dry ground again, surrounded by olive trees. It would take time, possibly a great deal of time, as Ham pointed out glumly.

Wherever it was that the little dove had found his olive leaf, we realised there was no guarantee that we would see that place ourselves at any time in the near future. It seemed even Father could not contain his impatience this time and he sent one of the doves out again a week later. This time, evening came and night fell and still the little bird did not return.

"Well I should think he feels pretty bad about that," said Ham, as we sat waiting for Father to join us for the evening meal.

"Shush Ham, I expect he does," said Nahlat hoping, as we all did, that Father hadn't heard him.

"Extinction ..." Ham whispered defiantly, snapping his fingers to emphasise his point.

At this Japhet began to laugh. "I know it's not funny and I shouldn't laugh, but I just can't help it."

"Oh for goodness sake you two, things are bad enough without you both setting Father off again," I said, digging Japhet hard in the ribs.

It wasn't simply boredom and growing impatience we had to contend with; we had very pressing concerns that food stocks were beginning to run worryingly low and the water we were drinking was getting unpleasantly brackish with a taste that is hard to describe: an unpalatable flavour of mud mixed with a weak solution of salt that made it almost undrinkable some days. Also, although I wouldn't have believed it possible, meal times seemed to have become even more monotonous; not surprising when we had the same food day after day, prepared from an increasingly limited supply of ingredients. Not even Mother and Arisisah's skills could disguise or vary it that much any more. Father often missed meals altogether and spent an increasing amount of time deep in prayer. As for the rest of us, with the workload mounting up again, we had to eat whatever was put in front of us to keep our strength up, whether or not we thought it was appetising.

We were all absolutely longing for this voyage to end and we constantly looked at the horizon or peered over the side of the ark hoping to see more than just fathomless water, but we never could. None of us were able to swim in deep water, because we had never needed to, but Japhet had an idea: why not send out an animal that

182

could swim to see if it could glean any information for us? The practicalities of putting his plan into action did at least engage and enthuse us all.

"What about a seal?" suggested Ham.

"A seal would never make it to the top of the ark and then how would we get it over the side? And then, if we did, how would we get it back on board again?" asked Japhet.

I had an idea: "If it can't get up to the deck and over the side, perhaps it could squeeze through one of the drainage outlets lower down?" The lowest outlets were not far above the water line and we no longer had to worry about flooding, as the sea had been calm for a long time now.

So that's what we tried. With great difficulty we managed to put a sling under the seal and lift it up into the water channel and then, with a good deal of pushing and shoving and dragging it along in the sling, we managed to move it up the channel to the outlet. Unfortunately after all our efforts it wouldn't fit right through the outlet; it was too fat. And worst of all, in our enthusiasm we had pushed it so hard through the hole that it was stuck half in and half out of the side of the ark. And then however hard we pushed, or pulled we didn't really have anything firm to grab hold of; its front flippers were pinned tightly to its sides in the outlet, which only left its tail flapping rather frenziedly at the end of its smooth-haired tapering body. By the time our hands had slipped that far down, we kept losing hold of it altogether.

"You know Father's going to be absolutely furious about this," I said, which didn't really help matters.

"Well, he had his birds, now we've got our seal," said Ham defiantly. "We're only doing our best to help after all."

"And anyway if we had got it out, how were we going to get it back on board?" said Japhet.

"We don't know!" said Ham and I in unison.

"Oh God, that's so irresponsible of you both, what are we going to do now?" asked Japhet.

"If we can't pull it back in from behind, maybe we could try pushing it in from the front," I suggested.

"And how do you think we are going to manage that?" asked Japhet scornfully.

"No, he's right," said Ham, "it's the only way. Shem's right about this." And he clapped me on the back. "So, are you volunteering then?"

And as the other two looked at me expectantly, I realised that since one of us would have to do the pushing, it looked as if it was going to be me.

"Just don't let Father find out," begged Japhet.

"No, there's no need for him to find out," I said.

"Where is he, though?" asked Ham. "If he's up on deck we've had it, because we'll have to lower you down from there."

"No, it'll be all right," I assured him. "He never goes on deck in the heat of the afternoon so he'll either be resting or praying, so don't worry. Let's just try not to draw attention to ourselves as we go through the ark."

We managed to get up on deck without anyone noticing us and when we looked over the side of the ark, we could see the unfortunate seal's head below us with its eyes protruding even more than usual. Its long black whiskers were drooping miserably and what could have been called its shoulders were stuck fast in the water outlet below its two flippers, which were wedged firmly by its side. I tied the rope round my waist and Ham and Japhet lowered me over the side, where I bumped uncomfortably over the pitch-covered planks, making slow progress down the side of the ark in fits and starts.

"Careful!" I yelled at one stage, but it was in vain. Ham and Japhet had been startled by the arrival of Arisisah and let the rope out too fast so I shot down past the seal, until I was almost dangling in the water.

"What on earth are you both doing?" I shouted up angrily, startled by my sudden rapid descent.

"Sorry," said Japhet, leaning over the side and looking down at me. "Are you there yet?"

"I'm more than there," I shouted back, "I've overshot the seal and it's at least two cubits above me now."

"Don't worry," Ham shouted down. "We'll just pull you back up a bit."

Finally I arrived at seal height and, looking at it eye to eye, it had an unmistakeably startled expression, which wasn't surprising in the circumstances. I tried patting it in a friendly but calming way but, as it couldn't move at all except to blink, it was hard to tell if this was a successful strategy or not.

"Oh just get on with it," Ham shouted down. "Father will be here soon if you don't hurry up."

I looked at the seal and it looked at me, hanging down by the side of it. Theoretically I needed to be in front of it, but then what? I couldn't just push it on the nose. I needed to assess the situation.

"I think someone ought to be on the inside at the other end," I shouted up.

"I'll go," Arisisah volunteered.

I gave her time to get there and then, instead of pushing directly from the front of the seal, which would have been difficult anyway; I tried easing him from one side and then the other. This made him try to wriggle away from me and for one awful moment I thought he was going to go the wrong way and pop out of the side of the ark into the water below and be lost forever. What I didn't know was that on the inside Arisisah had tied a rope round and round his tail, and then round a post, so that with my easing and her pulling, the seal finally slid back inside the ark and landed heavily in the water channel with a tremendous thump.

"Oh no, please don't let it collapse," wailed Arisisah, who knew how cross Japhet would be if it did and that Father was bound to ask how on earth it had happened. But fortunately the channel was strong enough to take the seal's weight and we managed to heave it out again and shoo it back to its enclosure before it did any damage.

185

"I don't think we'll try that again," I said once I had been hauled back up on deck.

"No, I don't think that was one of your best ideas," Arisisah agreed.

The Gods and the Idea of Monotheism
(Belief in Only One God)

Man, uniquely amongst all living creatures, seems to need to worship and perform rituals as a physical manifestation of his beliefs and none more so than those in the ancient Sumerian society of Mesopotamia. They believed that their wellbeing was utterly dependent on the goodwill of their numerous gods and that by worshipping these gods and making offerings to them, their lives would be made easier, with the gods ensuring good fortune, good weather and abundant crops.

Before the flood, people worshipped hundreds of different gods and it was never going to be easy to convince them to worship only one God, as Noah tried to do. To believe in one universal, all-seeing, supremely powerful God was asking for a huge leap of faith. How, they not unreasonably wondered, could just one God perform the duties of the hundreds of gods that they had always believed in before?

They believed their gods had human attributes and were of different status and hierarchy. They ranged from the lowly personal god, rather like the idea of a guardian angel, and progressed upward in importance.

Noah had difficulty getting his own family to believe his predictions and maybe some of them never did. In the Koran, it is said that Noah had four sons, including one who refused to believe or to act on the predictions of his Father. He refused to go on board the ark, preferring to sit on a mountain-top instead. He drowned.

There are no written records of the very first Mesopotamian gods but it is not unreasonable to assume that the sun (later known as Utu, the god of justice, who flooded the world with blinding light) and the moon (Nanna, the god who controlled time and the lunar months) were amongst them.

187

Later, following the flood, Noah's idea of one true God still had not taken hold and there were records of city gods who were important. But, reigning over all these gods, were the highest echelon of gods who were universally worshipped. For the Babylonians Marduk, his wife Zarpanitu, and his son Nabu, were commonly regarded as the most important of the gods and had been since nearly 2,000BC.

ഐᏣᏍᏖ

Chapter 20

❦

With no opportunity for exercise, with strange food and cramped conditions, the appearance of many of the animals had deteriorated badly. They no longer had the sleek glossy coats, vibrant feathers or shiny scales of the splendid beasts that we had originally chosen to take on board. The restricted life they led on the ark had taken its toll, and nearly all of them looked unkempt and shabby. And the animals that had stayed awake for most of the voyage were in even worse condition than the animals that had gone into hibernation.

"Oh no, just look at them all," Japhet sighed despondently. "You'd never think that we went to all that trouble to take the very best examples of their species with us, would you? Look over there at Enoch's ram; I remember I had my eye on him for ages, I had to throw in one of Father's best vines before I could persuade Enoch to even think of parting with him, and now look what a sorry sight he is."

"Oh, don't worry, he'll soon fatten up again when he gets some proper food," I said, trying to console him, although I had to admit that the ram was a shadow of his former splendid self. His horns seemed to be too big for his head, fronds of matted wool hung limply from his body, and his spindly legs ended in cloven hooves that were so long from lack of wear that they were beginning to turn up at the front.

"And have you seen the yaks lately?" Ham chipped in. "Their coats are matted with straw, hay and seed husks and there's nothing I can do. I think I'd rather try and groom a zebra than go anywhere near them. They're very handy with their horns, so until they moult naturally there's not much I can do for them."

"I hope we'll all fatten up," said Ham. "I feel famished most of the time. What's happened to the fish lately, Japhet, or have you been too busy looking after your animals?"

"Oh very funny. Actually I don't know the answer to that myself," said Japhet. "There just don't seem to be that many around at the moment, I can sit there for hours sometimes and catch nothing. I'm just not having much luck I suppose."

"Do you know," said Ham in a reflective tone, "just how fed up I am with being on the ark?"

"Do you think perhaps if we begged him, Father would let us cook one of the goats just for a change?" said Japhet suddenly. "There are several new kids now and I really can't see why one of them couldn't be spared."

"I'd say there's absolutely no chance," I said. "It would be too upsetting for the other animals. You know that's what he'll say."

"Not having any proper meat for so long is pretty upsetting for me," Ham grumbled, "and I don't count that revolting dried sandal leather that Mother served us as meat. When that ran out it was one of the highlights of the voyage, as far as I'm concerned.

"Do you know, I thought that the 40 days and nights would be it and then it would all be over," he suddenly said. "I forgot about the water, or rather the time it would take for the water to go down."

"Just imagine how much meat there would be on a zebra," mused Japhet.

"There'd be even more on an ox," I said.

"Or a yak. And still more on an elephant," said Ham. "Are you listening to me?"

"No, not really," admitted Japhet, "but they're not half as unpleasant as the zebras are, so they don't deserve to be eaten nearly as much." He was still having trouble with his black and white charges.

"Well I hate the flies above all," said Ham. "You remember I told Father right from the start that we should have left them out but, oh no, he didn't agree and look at us now – flies everywhere."

"But it would take an awful lot of flies to make a good meal," I said.

"Never mind a good meal, I'd just like to swat every single one of them and I really mean it," said Ham. "You are joking about eating them, I hope?" he said as an afterthought.

"Of course I am," I said, "killing them would be good enough for me; I wouldn't need to eat them as well."

At this, Ham and Japhet both looked at me strangely.

"What about one of the pandas?" suggested Japhet anxious to change the subject. "They still seem to dislike each other so much that I can't imagine there's going to be much hope for them breeding, so it wouldn't really matter, would it? In fact, maybe we could eat both of them."

"Well, what about one of the birds, then?" asked Ham, his imagination carried away by wishful thinking.

"Too small," said Japhet, "not enough meat on any of them to feed all of us."

"What about one of the ostriches? They're big with plenty of flesh on them," suggested Ham.

"I think they would be a bit conspicuous by their absence," said Japhet seriously.

"Never mind even thinking about it," I said, "because we all know that Father will never let us eat any of them, not before the ark lands anyway, so we'll just have to accept it."

"Oh well, I suppose you're right," said Japhet glumly.

"Isn't he always?" said Ham.

By now it wasn't just us men who were finding the whole situation increasingly stressful and monotonous. Even my dear Salit, normally so good-humoured and long suffering which is, of course, why I married her, was getting more irritable. Although to be fair, so far our wives had managed to cope with most things better than us men, by this stage even they were tired of the lack of privacy, the confined space and seeing so little of their husbands except at meal times.

Of our three wives, only Nahlat had any real experience of

191

travelling before the ark. As the youngest daughter of a successful farmer, she had made the long journey to marry Ham, further than the rest of us put together had ever travelled. Salit and her family had lived quite close to us, in very similar circumstances, and Arisisah was a real country girl who was used to moving around the local area with her family's flocks and living in tents as they went from pasture to pasture, but had never really ventured very far afield.

Once married into our family, all three of them had led lives that totally revolved around our home, but even so they had still had friends and the opportunity to walk about in the village. After so long floating about in the ark, they missed their old life more and more.

Following our futile efforts with the seal and subsequent failed attempts with bits of rope knotted together that wouldn't sink because we had nothing onboard that could be spared to weigh them down, we lost all interest in measuring the depth of the waters we were sailing in. If we hadn't, perhaps our next sight of land would not have come as such a tremendous surprise to us all. This time, it was not just a small rock or two sticking out of the water: we woke to find a huge mountain range looming ahead of us and the ark slowly floating towards a shallow inland lake lying at the foot of it.

Father was the first to see land. He had risen early to pray and when he stepped on deck he saw the huge mountain range in the distance. For some reason he decided it would be best to let us sleep on and see it in our own time.

When Mother rose she had a very different opinion on her husband's silence and dared to scold him. "After all this time Husband, don't you think we would all have risen from our beds at any time of the day or night to see land again? Don't you realise that we are all absolutely desperate to walk on firm ground again? And yet you decide to let us all sleep on. Sometimes I just don't understand you."

On hearing the argument, we all rose to see what was going on.

"What's the matter?" Nahlat asked sleepily, woken by Mother's hot words.

"Oh, nothing," said Ham ."It's only Father telling Mother that there is land in sight."

"LAND!" screamed Nahlat. "LAND?" and with that she jumped from her bed and shot straight up the nearest ladder to the deck.

"What are we going to do?" sighed Arisisah when she saw it. "It seems so far away still. Supposing we just float away again?"

"Just wait I suppose," said Ham.

"She's right, supposing we just sail on past it, like we did with the rocks?" said Nahlat.

I'm sure ideas of wading towards it came to all our minds and, as if he could read them, Father spoke, raising his hand to catch everyone's attention.

"Just be calm please everyone. Land, as you can see, is in sight and very nearly in touch. Be patient all of you and don't do anything foolish."

So there we were, our first real sight of land for over a year, and not just a small bit of land, but a huge, towering, craggy mountain range so high that the tops were almost out of sight. The two small rocks that had briefly appeared and then vanished as we passed them hardly counted in comparison to what we had before us now.

I couldn't see anything about the land that had changed from how it looked before. Everything was as we would have expected. The vegetation at ground level had the fresh green look of new growth and the higher up you looked, the less green there was. Improbably, right up near the top of the mountain slopes, a few sapling trees appeared to have survived the flood; they of course would have been under water for less time than the vegetation lower down.

There was a lot of detritus along the shores of the lake, but it was hard to see what it was as we were still too far away.

"Bones, I expect," was Ham's ghoulish contribution.

Father calmed us down by saying it was far more likely to be bleached wood from submerged trees.

"Father...?" began Japhet, "shall we open the roof right up now, and then at least the birds can go free?"

"An excellent idea. I can see no reason why not. Will you see to it, then?"

"Certainly, Father, I'll go right now."

We didn't need telling twice. Racing up to the top deck we began to dismantle the covering from the entire roof, throwing bits of timber spiralling down into the waters around the ark.

The very first birds to leave the ark were the kingfishers, two rainbow darts flashing like metal in the sunlight as they shot off. With such a large chunk of land in sight there were plenty of perching places for the birds and they sensed freedom at last.

In particular I noticed that the dove that had been left behind was so anxious to leave and find her mate that she squeezed out of one of the larger holes in the roof as fast as she could. As the whole roof of the ark gradually came off, the noise level rose to a cacophony of sound: screeching, hooting, excited twitters, harsh cries and gentle coos from the huge variety of birds who had spent the voyage perched above us.

Then came the sound of their wings, like a muffled roar above us; they rose in a multi-coloured cloud from the perching poles and soared skywards. How we envied their ability to escape the confines of the ark as we watched them whirl in rainbow circles above us, before finally flying inland towards the shore of the lake. As they arrived at the shallow water on the edge of the lake nearly all of them stopped to sip the water, dipping their heads down and then throwing them back to let the water trickle down their throats. Some bathed as well, fluffing out their feathers like puff-balls, delighted to be released from the gloom and dust of the ark.

But we were still trapped on board, humans and animals, while the ark drifted tantalisingly slowly towards the shore. And disappointingly, by the end of the day, we were still some way out and Father told us to carry on with things as usual and hope that by the following morning we would be near enough to the shore to disembark.

Not surprisingly, the sounds of the roof being removed and the pandemonium caused by the birds' noisy departure had unsettled many of the animals. Inside the ark there was an air of tension and pent up energy. Even normally docile animals acted restlessly and the more highly-strung creatures began to swirl and fidget about in their stalls, much as they had when the storms were at their most violent. Fortunately, we were able to distract most of them by feeding them liberal amounts of food from the remaining supplies and they began to settle down again.

Poor Japhet was outraged that the female zebra had managed to kick him one last time and Ham was concerned that the elephants and larger animals might panic and run amok in a final bid for freedom. The dodos still waddled unperturbed down the passageways together, quite oblivious to any danger or excitement around them, appearing to have no instinct for self-preservation at all.

"I just don't know how those two have survived the voyage," said Ham. "I have never seen such stupid creatures do look at them both. When the gangplank goes down they'll be trampled to death in the rush if they don't watch out."

As there was a very high probability of this happening, I caught hold of the two dodos by their stubby wings and shut them in an empty stall out of harm's way. I knew they wouldn't be forgotten because they had a very unusual honking kind of cry that couldn't help but catch someone's attention when things quietened down again.

As darkness fell over the mountains and the lake, we finally got a chance to relax, sitting out on the open deck while Father played his flute for us, as he had done on so many previous evenings. The effect of his playing was as calming as ever and our impatience at the delay just seemed to drift away over the lake with the notes. I put my arm around Salit's shoulders and together we looked up at the night sky, listening to Father and the gentle lap of the water as the ark floated slowly and serenely towards the land in the final hours of our voyage.

The Final Resting Place

No one can say for certain where the ark finally came to rest when the waters of the flood subsided. Claims have been made for at least nine locations, ranging from Asia Minor to Afghanistan and Armenia. Early Christian and Jewish scholars identified Mount Quardu (now called Jabal Judi) in Arabia.

Various locations in and around Mesopotamia have been said to be the site, but it has proved impossible to verify any of them. This is not unusual and many other iconic settings and objects have never been found, including the Garden of Eden, the Hanging Gardens of Babylon, the tablets of the Ten Commandments and the Ark of the Covenant, the wooden chest that may once have held them.

More recently, claims have been made for Mount Ararat in the Turkish Agri Dagi Massif, 17,000–feet high, as the ark's resting place. This location has a strange rock formation which, it has been suggested, is the ark petrified – its wood turned to stone. And whilst it does look like the remains of a large boat, expert geologists agree that it is more than likely that this is a purely incidental freak of nature. Of course, any neighbourhood that can claim the possibility of being close to the site of a great historical event or biblical story would benefit hugely from tourist trade, so there are many claims. The presence of swimming cats in Lake Van near Mount Ararat adds to the allure, if not to the veracity, of this location.

Ararat was the biblical name for the country of Assyrian Urartu in eastern Asia Minor, in nearly 1,000BC, which encompassed parts of Turkey, Armenia, Iran and Iraq. Over hundreds of years and after various battles it was finally incorporated into the Persian Empire.

Rather than coming to rest on a highly unsuitable mountain top, it is likely that the ark came to rest in one of the valleys of that area, now western Turkey or eastern Iran. Any of these would have been a far more likely location considering the practicalities of disembarking hundreds of animals and birds.

God does not appear to put great store in the preservation of religious icons to help men believe and may have reasoned that if a man will not believe in the word of God as preached by his prophets, why should he be convinced by any physical object? Indeed, claims about religious icons such as wood from the cross, the Turin Shroud and so on are more often greeted with scepticism than reverence.

᭡᭡᭡

Chapter 21

❧

By the next morning we were close to the shore at last and could finally see the bed of the lake through the clear water below the ark. Now it was the turn of the water birds to leave. The ducks and herons were amongst the first, balancing daringly on the side of the ark before launching into the water below and, amazingly, of all the other animals, the cats were the first to follow them over.

"They must be as desperate for meat as I am," said Ham.

And as we watched, one of the cats pounced on a duck while it was still in the shallows and killed it.

"Oh God!" said Japhet, who was rather squeamish.

"Extinction," muttered Ham, who was not.

Then the small water animals started to go over the edge, too. Some were amazingly brave for their size and others teetered and dithered for ages before finally plucking up courage and jumping or slipping and slithering overboard. By now, some of the more resourceful animals and birds had realised they could also escape through the water inlets lower down. Very soon the water below us was alive with the bobbing heads of swimming animals large and small.

"Carnage ahead," said Ham with pretend gusto.

"I never realised just how many lemmings there were," said Arisisah with wonder, as a herd of small furry beasts streamed past us like a living carpet, before making their way up and over the side in a mad scramble and plopping down into the shallows far below like a hail of pebbles.

Meanwhile, our wives busied themselves in the living quarters, packing the last of our belongings into bags and hauling them down to the central area below, where the gangplank would finally be lowered down.

"That is if Father can ever make up his mind to get on with it," said Japhet in exasperation.

"Surely we could let the gangplank down now, Father?" pleaded Nahlat. "A little water won't hurt any of us."

But right to the last Father remained cautious; he decided we were still too far from shore and it would be better to wait until we were absolutely sure that we could lower the gangplank safely. But as the increasing frenzy of excitement amongst the waiting animals grew, and some of them started plunging and whirling around in their stalls to such an extent that they were in danger of injuring themselves, he was finally forced to give the order to lower the gangplank. Due to the depth of the water it was at a much steeper angle than Father would have chosen, and more like a slide.

The exit from the ark was absolute chaos, just as Father had feared, but his worries about the depth of the water around the ark turned out to be a good thing. With the water still quite deep at the bottom of the gangplank, some of the disembarking animals hesitated just a little, before plunging down it. Their natural caution prevented them from rushing down the plank regardless and trampling on each other. Had it not, I'm sure that many of them would have been injured or drowned.

Even so, when the great planks first splashed down into the water, it took all our efforts to prevent pandemonium amongst the now-frenzied beasts. The largest animals went off first, mainly because it would have been quite impossible to stop them. By now they were absolutely desperate to get to the freedom of land and some of them were so excited that they broke out of their stalls before we could release them.

And what a motley lot they looked as they scrambled past us. Their time in such unnatural conditions had dulled their handsome coats and their eyes watered and blinked in the full glare of daylight. The sudden change must have been a great shock for them all. The ark reverberated with the sound of hoof beats, squeals and the noise of overexcited and nervous animals all vying for position. The gangplank became more and more slippery as they slid and skidded down it and into the water. But by now there was absolutely nothing we could have done to slow them down, so we just had to let them get on with it. Most of them did get down the gangplank safely, with surprisingly few slipping or falling into the water.

Once the largest animals such as the elephants, hippos and rhinoceroses had barged off, quite out of our control, we were able to organise the exit of the smaller animals a little bit more safely. Then, of course, there were some animals like the giraffes that held up the proceedings by refusing to move or go anywhere.

"Get them back out of the way then," shouted Ham. "We'll try with them later."

So we stopped pushing and pulling the tall, gentle beasts and let them remain behind, timidly swaying from side to side, like a couple of tall trees in the middle of the ark. The smaller animals just had to rush around them and some even shot between their legs in their final break for freedom. There was no budging the two giraffes until things had calmed down and they felt more confident.

"Personally I think this could have been organised a lot better," said Japhet, standing back as the throng of animals continued to surge past us down the gangplank. "Whatever happens, we must stop the smallest animals from getting mixed up in this. They'll be squashed to pieces and then all our work to keep them alive will have been in vain."

"Don't worry," I said. "Mother has already gone back up to the middle deck with Salit and Nahlat and they are doing pretty well in stopping the smaller animals from coming down too soon and getting hurt in the throng."

Finally, as the last of the larger animals departed, the animals from the middle deck couldn't be restrained any longer and started to push and wriggle their way down the interior gangways, even forcing their way down the food chutes. There was quite a lot of biting and snapping and the noise of hundreds of small feet drumming on the floor as they made their way down to the gangplank. Many of the smaller animals in particular, such as the rabbits and guinea pigs, had passed their voyage breeding successfully and now scuttled past us in droves. Having been made to wait until last to be released, many of them fell off the sides of the gangplank in their anxiety to leave and to our horror the crocodiles and alligators that had been lurking in the shallows around the gangplank snapped them up.

"And look up there," said Japhet pointing to shore. "Some things never change." We could see the pair of vultures, eyes following the proceedings intently, quietly sitting in the rocks overlooking the scene just waiting for their chance.

"Look over there at the hyenas," said Ham pointing to the animals as they splashed ashore. They were skulking about in their sinister way, biding their time, and just looking for any signs of weakness or injury that they might profit from.

The giraffes had finally been persuaded to make their way out of the ark and down the gangplank. Once they reached land they did not wait around with the other animals but immediately started to gallop away towards the distant plains with their strange rolling gait. The zebras and some of the gazelles, seeing them go, swerved away from the main group and followed after them with a thunder of hooves and clouds of dust, some of them bucking with excitement as they went. I couldn't help feeling a little sad to see them go; we hadn't seen anything like them before all this and I doubted that we would ever see anything like them again.

But in spite of the turmoil and commotion, in the general rush to get off the ark and reach the shore there were still a few stragglers, and even some animals that had managed to sleep through it all. Japhet and I, with the help of our wives, checked all the stalls, felt amongst the straw and woke some of the sleeping mice and snakes and even the odd large animal, such as the huge brown bears, that had been fast asleep for most of the voyage.

"I don't know how they sleep through all this noise," said Japhet. "It's amazing. We'd better look out now though, they're awake." But although they were awake they must have felt disorientated because instead of following all the other animals off the ark they did the opposite. They came out of their stall, wheeled around and shot off up to the middle deck.

"Damnation, I'm not sure if the gangplank will hold them up there," Japhet yelled. "Couldn't you have stopped them?" he asked no one in particular.

We realised they were searching for food; they were obviously ravenous after so long a sleep, and had set about ripping the few remaining food sacks to shreds and devouring the contents before we could do anything to get them off the ark.

Finally there were the two yetis, strange creatures that they were, still huddled away from the rest of us in the bow of the ark. They were awake but still crouching down out of sight, where we might well have forgotten them. Apart from all the hair and their great height, they were so like us that we always felt we should treat them with rather more deference than the other animals. We had to gently coax them out of their lair, where they stood cowering in the unaccustomed light, blinking at the huge door of the ark and in the end we had to walk arm in arm with them to the top of the gangway, and then part of the way down it, before they seemed to grasp what was happening. When they saw all the rest of the animals onshore, they suddenly took off down the gangplank, waded through the shallows and made their way through the herds of animals before heading straight for the mountains.

Despite our longing to be on land as much as any of the animals, the family had to be the very last to leave the ark, dragging our belongings down behind us, with Mother insisting that we absolutely must keep everything dry, which was impossible. Our greatest concern was keeping out of the way of the crocodiles, so we were all mightily relieved when Japhet pointed out that they had finally moved quite a distance away and were sunning themselves on some sandbanks, looking sated.

We heaved our last belongings to shore and slumped to the ground exhausted.

"What a day," said Father prodding at the earth with his staff as he waded ashore. "I am sure God will think we've all done our best. And for that I must thank you, each and every one of you, for the part you have played in this great endeavour. Now, I think I will just leave you all for a while." With that he rapidly made his way through all the animals, towards the foot of the nearest mountain – to pray of course.

The anticipation of a more varied diet had been a dream for all of us and it wasn't long before we all voiced our desire to make it a reality.

"What are we going to eat then?" said Ham with gusto. "Or should it be who? I certainly wouldn't mind if I never ate another lentil or grain of rice or slice of flatbread again and I'm not so keen on fish any more either."

Whether it was Ham's words or just coincidental timing, the huge group of animals that had been milling around us nibbling the grass or simply standing around contentedly, started to disperse. Some of them sheered off from the main group and galloped away towards the plains to the West, following the giraffes. And others such as the pandas, small-eared elephants and tigers walked off in stately manner towards the East; a group of the white animals, the bears, foxes, yaks and penguins, set off at a steady pace further into the mountains in a Northerly direction.

But not all of the animals deserted us; those that we had looked after before going onto the ark still seemed quite happy to stay, contentedly grazing around us or wandering about nearby.

"Habit," said Japhet knowledgeably.

"Well, thank God for habit, then," said Ham. "I don't think I could bear watching our next meal gallop off into the mountains."

The dogs lay panting in the nearest shade and the goats and sheep stayed together in a small flock, while the camels leant down at the edge of the water and drank and drank. Watching them, I felt more than relieved that supplying them with a refill would no longer be up to us. None of us really knew what to do next and we were so tired that in the end we decided we had better wait for Father's return before we did anything very much, certainly before butchering one of the animals. I was relieved as it gave us a chance to rest after what had been a very exhausting and emotional start to the day.

Having had a brief look round the clearing above the beach, we all concentrated on making ourselves as comfortable as we could and finding shady places to sit or lie down. Nobody said very much. But, before long, Ham had a suggestion: "Don't you think?" he said, "that Father would be pleased if he came back and found a nice cooked chicken or two waiting for him?"

"Or a roasted sheep, maybe?" Japhet suggested hopefully.

The very thought of such gastronomic delights made my mouth water, but unfortunately Mother disagreed and said firmly: "No, we must wait for his return." So Ham and Japhet amused themselves by choosing which of the animals they would cook as soon as they had the chance and I pottered around looking for somewhere suitable for us all to set up camp for the night.

It was strange how easily we adapted to being back on dry land, in spite of having no home, but it was stranger still to realise that everyone and everything that we had known before the flood had gone and we would never see any of them again. We had no idea where we were and, although we could tell a lot from the rising and the setting of the sun, we had no idea how far we were from where we had started. Only Ham and Nahlat had any experience of places other than our village and its surroundings and neither of them recognised the shape of the mountain range around us.

"What are you doing, Shem?" shouted Japhet. "It's hot, come and sit down."

"It's all right, I'm looking for somewhere suitable for us to camp tonight," I called back.

"Well, not there," shouted Ham. "With the vultures perched right above us I wouldn't be able to sleep."

And while I thought the chances of our being kept awake by

anything were highly unlikely, I suppose he did have a point. Sure enough, there sat the two vultures, immobile except for their eyes, which were constantly moving from side to side, alert to any signs of movement. And of course once he had pointed this out, there was a chorus of "No, not there, Shem," from everyone else.

After the Flood

We are told that God sent the flood as a punishment to purify a world that was full of sin. But, once the survivors and their descendants settled down and life got back to some semblance of normal, there was no lasting improvement in their behaviour. Indeed, very shortly after the flood, before any memory of the horrors could have been forgotten, several instances of poor behaviour are described in the Bible and these involved Noah's own family.

The first was Ham's regrettable shaming of his Father who he found drunk and naked in his tent. The anger and recrimination following this incident finally brought about the departure of the sons from the original landing place by the lake, where Noah remained.

Then, in spite of God's wish that the sons and descendants of Noah should go forth and multiply and fill the earth, we read that they didn't disperse but settled down together in the region of Sumer, building the world's first great city, Babylon. It was here that the huge temple was built to honour Marduk, the mythical god of the Babylonian state. So much for Noah's one God ...

Although Shem's descendants did finally spread out, settling down in the region of Mesopotamia, Ham's in Canaan, Egypt and Northern Africa and Japhet's further afield in Asia (today's Turkey), Greece and central Europe, this did not happen until God took action to encourage them to disperse.

In spite of many subsequent world disasters, wars, famines, floods and fires, generally people have been reluctant to attribute them to a vengeful God and instead hold them up as evidence of the wickedness of man. Perhaps in part this is because it is uncomfortable and frightening to accept that God has such power.

☙❦❧

Chapter 22

❖

While Father was away, I spent my time fruitlessly looking around for a suitable location to set up camp for the night but, in spite of my endeavours, nowhere I suggested seemed to please everyone. By the time Father returned, we had still been unable to agree on anywhere that was acceptable to all of us.

When Father reappeared I think all of us felt a shiver of apprehension when we saw his serious expression. Had God given him another enormous task? And, if he had, would it be something that involved all of us? Would we have another colossal project to cope with? I said a quick and heartfelt prayer begging that would not be the case. Looking at Father, Arisisah began to cry and was comforted by Mother and Salit. It was Nahlat who finally plucked up the courage to ask him: "What now, Father?"

"Wife, sons, daughters, there is no need for any of you to fear; I have no more bad news for you. I have prayed and built an altar so now we must sacrifice offerings of fowls and other sacramental creatures, to honour and thank the Lord for our safe deliverance to this place."

"Well, that's a relief," said Ham, "we can cope with that." And he looked around for confirmation that the rest of us agreed with him, which we did.

While the men built a small fire at Father's rudimentary altar and burnt the sacrifices according to Father's directions, our wives withdrew to a distance. Then, rather terrifyingly, God made his promises aloud to all four of us. So this time when he spoke to Father we, his three sons, all heard the voice of God directly for the first time. He had much to say and we all knelt in awe at the sound of his voice. I could not have stood upright;

my legs were trembling so much. After this we returned to our wives, still stunned by what had just happened and, for once, they did not immediately pester us with questions, but waited patiently to hear what we had to say.

"Where to start?" said Ham, who was the first of us to recover his equilibrium.

"Sons, daughters, Wife," said Father taking over and holding his hand up for silence. "We are to multiply and our children and descendants will occupy the earth."

"We are to be the custodians of all the animals and birds and fish, and they will fear us," blurted out Japhet.

"And every man who kills another should be killed in his turn, because man is made in the image of God. To kill a man is to kill part of God," said Ham, anxious to show that he too had remembered and understood what had been said.

"And, most important, in the circumstances," I added, "there will never be another flood like this one."

But before I could go on everyone interrupted, cheering enthusiastically at what I had just said, some of them even shedding tears of relief.

"And God has promised to give us a sign of this promise, which will stop us all worrying every time it rains," I continued. "The sign will be a rainbow; that will remind both God, man and the animals and creatures of the earth and sea that he has promised he will never again send a flood to destroy his creation."

"Well done, Shem," said Father. "Well put."

"What's a rainbow?" asked Nahlat.

We all turned to look at her questioningly.

Then Father broke the silence: "Daughter, that's a rainbow." And he pointed to where a shimmering arch of colour had appeared over the far shore of the lake.

For some time after our deliverance we all lived along the shores of the lake, not far from the spot where we had landed, using wood from the ark to make liveable dwellings and establishing a new community. Before long the shores of the lake rang to the excited cries of our children, Noah's grandchildren. We immediately started growing crops with seed from the ark and breeding from our animals to replenish our supplies. And, of course, Father established a vineyard with his precious vines. However, things never went back to the way they had been before the ark. Since then we had experienced so much that, although we tried, it was hard to settle back into our old ways.

Our living together in harmony came to an end when Ham made one joke too many at Father's expense; this time Father would not ignore it and was so angry when he discovered that Ham had made fun of him when he was drunk that he cursed Ham's son Canaan, which was far more terrible than cursing Ham himself. Sadly, that was the end of us all living together.

Father never travelled again, but the rest of us had to move on. Apart from the bad feeling that now existed between Ham and Father, by now there were so many of us that the land around the lake could no longer provide enough food for everyone. The water receded more and more and the animals from the ark that remained with us thrived and increased hugely in number. So by the time we left, there was enough livestock for each of us to take some animals with us.

At first we all resettled together and we stayed together for many years; our families, and then their families, grew and grew and together we all flourished. But we had forgotten one of God's wishes: that we should disperse and spread all over the earth. Together we were amongst the founders of the great city of Babylon and there we would happily have stayed, but the strangest thing happened ... One day no one could understand what anyone else was saying. It was quite unexpected, incredibly frustrating and rather frightening.

We couldn't communicate our ideas about what to do until finally someone drew in the sand with a stick a picture featuring men walking and arrows facing in all directions.

Then it slowly dawned on everyone that leaving Father had not been enough. This babble of language, which made families incomprehensible to each other, was God's way of telling us to move on. It was quite heartbreaking for us to separate, but we knew what had to be done. There were tears and tantrums, but by now we knew better than to ignore the word of God. Ham's descendants went to the West; Japhet's to the East and now only my family still remains close to where we started out.

Although his three sons moved on, Father had decided to stay put. He was happy enough with his vineyard in the foothills of the mountains, with his animals grazing around the lake and Mother to keep him company. He had no desire to leave. He told us that at that stage of his life, after everything that we had been through, he had all that he wanted or needed to live in peace and comfort until the end of his days.

But for the rest of us, our lives were just beginning ...